PENGUIN SHORT FICTION

"Not that the story need be long, but it
will take a long while to make it short."
–Henry David Thoreau

THE THRILL OF THE GRASS

Born in Edmonton, Alberta, W.P. Kinsella has been writing
stories since he was a young child. He has also worked as a
civil servant, a life insurance salesman, a cab driver, a pizza-
parlour manager and a teacher of creative writing. He
earned a B.A. at the University of Victoria in 1974 and an
M.F.A. at the University of Iowa in 1978. Kinsella and his
wife, Ann, now live in White Rock, B.C.

Shoeless Joe, W.P. Kinsella's first novel, was published in
1982 to critical acclaim and won several awards, including
the Houghton Mifflin Literary Fellowship and the *Books in
Canada* First Novel Award. It was also made into a widely-
praised film, *Field of Dreams* (1989). Other published work
by the author includes *Dance Me Outside* (1977), *Scars*
(1978), *Shoeless Joe Jackson Comes to Iowa* (1980), *Born
Indian* (1981), *Shoeless Joe* (1982), *The Moccasin Telegraph*
(1983), *The Alligator Report* (1985), *The Iowa Baseball
Confederacy* (1986), *The Fencepost Chronicles* (1986), *Red
Wolf, Red Wolf* (1987), *The Further Adventures of Slugger
McBat* (1988), *The Miss Hobbema Pageant* (1989) and *The
Dixon Cornbelt League* (1992).

THE THRILL OF THE GRASS

W. P. Kinsella

Penguin Books

PENGUIN BOOKS

Published by the Penguin Group

Penguin Books Canada Ltd, 10 Alcorn Avenue, Toronto, Ontario, Canada M4V 3B2

Penguin Books Ltd, 27 Wrights Lane, London W8 5TZ, England

Penguin Books USA Inc., 375 Hudson Street, New York, New York 10014, U.S.A.

Penguin Books Australia Ltd, Ringwood, Victoria, Australia

Penguin Books (NZ) Ltd, 182-190 Wairau Road, Auckland 10, New Zealand

Penguin Books Ltd, Registered Offices:
Harmondsworth, Middlesex, England

Published in Penguin Books, 1984

11 13 15 17 19 20 18 16 14 12

Copyright © W.P. Kinsella, 1984

All rights reserved

Manufactured in Canada

Series design by David Wyman

Canadian Cataloguing in Publication Data
Kinsella, W.P.
The thrill of the grass

(Penguin short fiction)
ISBN 0-14-007386-8

I. Title. II. Series.

PS8571.I57T57 1984   C813'.54   C84-098292-5
PR9199.3.K59T57 1984

For Bev

Acknowledgements

"The Baseball Spur" first appeared in *Descant*

"How I Got My Nickname" first appeared in
Spitball

"Nursie" first appeared in *The Spirit That Moves Us*

"The Night Manny Mota Tied the Record" first
appeared on *CBC Anthology* and *Small Wonders*

"Driving Toward the Moon" first appeared in
NeWest ReView

"Barefoot and Pregnant in Des Moines" first
appeared in *The Virginia Quarterly Review*

"The Firefighter" first appeared in *Watershed*

"The Thrill of the Grass" first appeared on *CBC
Anthology* and *CBC Storyline* and was also published as
a chapbook by William Hoffer Standard Editions

Contents

Introduction   ix

The Last Pennant Before Armageddon   1

The Baseball Spur   23

How I Got My Nickname   47

Bud and Tom   61

Nursie   77

The Night Manny Mota Tied the Record   91

Driving Toward the Moon   107

Barefoot and Pregnant in Des Moines   129

The Firefighter   141

The Battery   163

The Thrill of the Grass   185

Introduction

"Where do stories come from?" That, and, "How much is autobiography?" are the questions I am most frequently asked. I don't understand readers' morbid fascination with autobiography in fiction. For some reason readers want the author to really be the character he writes about. It's called The Implied Author Syndrome, and I've fallen victim to it a few times myself. Because of the wide variety of fiction I write, my cumulative Implied Author would be an Indian baseball fanatic who practices magic, has kidnapped J.D. Salinger and made love to Janis Joplin. In reality I am a middle-aged writer who likes to stare at the ocean or the Iowa corn fields while I create works of imagination. My protagonists are usually good-natured, compassionate, somewhat befuddled by the curves life has thrown at them, but always aware, to varying degrees, that the world is a totally absurd place.

Perhaps the absurdity is where autobiography enters my work, for while I am much more cynical than my characters, much angrier, I am always very conscious of the absurdity that surrounds me.

Everyone who takes themselves too seriously is absurd:

politicians, religious leaders, academics, activists of every ilk. It is my observation that almost without exception, incompetent people are in positions of power. Society survives because of luck, not good management.

A writer can't help but toss little morsels of himself into his stories: I once collected a cupful of cherry blossoms from the streets of Victoria and left them by the bedside of my sleeping daughter; I once shot a sparrow and brought it to my mother expecting approval; I was once humiliated by a carnival barker; I have a delicious red-headed wife named Ann who is ultra-supportive of my career. These items appeared in various forms in my novel *Shoeless Joe*, but they were mere snippets of truth; I had to invent the rest. Much fiction fails because it is autobiographical, the lives of ninety percent of the population are so dull that no one would care in the least about them, the lives of the remaining ten percent are so bizarre that no one would believe them. A writer must liven up the dull, tone down the bizarre until it is believable.

Invention is what fiction writing is all about. It is also making the unusual believable. It doesn't matter in the least what the writer knows about a subject, if he can make a reader say, "Yes, I believe that's the way it is," then the writing is successful.

Someone once said, "Those who never attempt the absurd never achieve the impossible." I like to keep attempting the impossible. I like to do audacious things. I like to weave fact and fantasy. I like to alter history.

But first and foremost I am a storyteller. My greatest criticism of modern fiction is that writers tend to forget they are storytellers, entertainers. Readers allow for boredom, even expect to be bored when they read nonfiction, because they ultimately expect to learn something. The storyteller's craft evolves from the time when the tribe sat around the campfire in the evening and someone decided he wanted to brag about his hunting exploits. "Listen to me!" he said. "I want to tell you a story."

If that story was not colourful and entertaining the audience very soon disappeared. As it should be. A writer's first duty is to entertain. If something profound, symbolic, or philosophical can be slipped in, along with the entertainment, so much the better. But if the element of entertainment is not there, the writing becomes treatise, essay, or autobiography, and the writer has no right to call it fiction. Ultimately, a fiction writer can be anything except boring.

A number of the stories in this collection deal with magical happenings. When these stories work well it is because the storyteller takes over and the author disappears. Interviewers have tried, always unsuccessfully, to make me admit I believe in the magic I write about. The very idea is ludicrous. Writers who, like Alfred Jarry, begin to believe their fantastical fiction is truth, end up prematurely dead.

I think that when my magical stories work, it is because I have no illusions about magic. I know fiction when I create it. I am a realist. There are no gods. There is no magic. I may be a wizard, though, for it takes a wizard to know there are none.

Where do stories come from? Usually from some snippet of information I read in a newspaper, magazine, other author's work, from TV, or overheard conversation. I saw a three line filler in a newspaper stating that the President of the Dominican Republic had bestowed some ludicrous title, like Knight Commander of the Blue Camellia, on Juan Marichal, to honour his induction into the Baseball Hall of Fame. From that grew the story "The Battery."

While I was on a promotional tour for *Shoeless Joe*, I appeared on a sports call-in show in Milwaukee, and a caller suggested the idea of long-dead Chicago Cub fans lobbying God to allow the Cubs to win a pennant. From that came "The Last Pennant Before Armageddon." I don't even know if the caller will recognize his idea. Perhaps I'll hear from him.

"The Thrill of the Grass," came from a line in *Shoeless Joe*, when Joe Jackson says "I'd wake in the night with the smell of the ballpark in my nose and the cool of the grass on my feet. The thrill of the grass." I combined that idea with my opposition to artificial turf. Of course, the idea of breaking into a baseball stadium was first explored in Hugh Hood's marvellous story "Ghosts at Jarry."

A friend and fellow writer, Anthony Bukoski, told me a story about there being a baseball spur in a freight yard, perhaps in his home town of Superior, Wisconsin. I begged him to let me use the idea. He did.

I was present in Los Angeles, the night Manny Mota tied the record for most pinch hits. My wife brought me my favourite ice cream to soften the blow of Thurman Munson's death. In Met Stadium in Minneapolis I once sat behind a group of people very similar to The Buffalo Brigade. I simply shook all the ingredients and a story came out.

I once read an article about Red Adair the world-famous oilfield firefighter. I said, "What if," which is what writers spend all their lives saying, "What if I invented a poor, incompetent, egomaniacial, $1.98 version of Red Adair?" From that came "The Firefighter."

The stories in this collection all have to do with some facet of baseball. There is little of the two-out-last-of-the-ninth-hero-must-get-a-hit-or-pitcher-must-strike-out-the-side, heroics. I personally find that kind of fiction boring. Stories that get intimately involved in play-by-play usually fail.

I am often asked about the relationship of baseball and magic. I feel it is the timelessness of baseball which makes it more conducive to magical happenings than any other sport. There are forays into magic, but I also realize baseball players are very ordinary mortals with the same financial, and domestic problems as Joe Citizen. As well, they suffer unique problems because of the short and ephemeral nature of their careers. Every player, no matter his talent, is only one beanball or one torn rotator-cuff away from the past tense.

For those who prefer to seek below the surface searching for hidden meaning, there are symbols, ironies, Biblical and mythological tales retold. But first and always these stories were written to entertain.

"Hey! Listen to me! I want to tell you a story . . ."

The Last Pennant
Before Armageddon

The Last Pennant
Before Armageddon

MONTHS LATER, after the cycle of dreams began their nightly invasion of his body, Al Tiller recalled the night the archangel had telephoned the radio station, and he realized that then, and not on the evening of the first dream, was when his troubles had started.

In September, with eighteen games left to play, with the Chicago Cubs holding a full five-game lead in the Eastern Division of the National League, with the Cubs, tired after the long pennant race, playing only .500 baseball since mid-August, but with their chief rivals for the pennant — Montreal and Philadelphia — matching them loss for loss, Al "the Hun" Tiller should have been the happiest man and manager in the world. He was leading the Cubbies toward a first-place finish. If they succeeded it would be the first time the Cubs had won anything since 1945. Al Tiller's lopsided smile stared out from the covers of *Time* and *Sports Illustrated* that week. But instead of being happy Al Tiller found himself waking in the night with the black sweats, trembling like a rookie, his heart thudding as if it were being used as a drum.

Al Tiller was overwhelmed by the mysteries of life, knowing

things he felt he had no right to know. His only desire was to manage his baseball team in an honourable manner; he did not want to be entrusted with monumental secrets. Unfortunately, he could not stop the information from coming to him. He could not turn away, or hang up the phone, or tear up a letter.

I'd as soon be carrying around the Mafia's account records, or ten pounds of heroin, as know what I know, Al Tiller thought.

He could not share his burden with anyone. Baseball managers are very lonely people. He certainly couldn't tell the press. Sportswriters had been making enough snide remarks about him anyway without his letting it be known that he was having apocalyptic dreams.

"The sun is finally shining on Al Tiller," read a recent headline in the *Trib.* For the moment he was the most famous baseball manager in the nation, the man guiding the Chicago Cubs toward their first pennant in half a century; everyone wanted to talk baseball, no one gave a damn about his dreams.

He could picture himself at a news conference, pausing right in the middle of fielding questions about his pitching rotation and his left fielder's Achilles tendon, to say, "Gentlemen, for the past several weeks I have been having prophetic dreams. It is my considered opinion that if the Chicago Cubs win the National League pennant, the world is going to end."

He knew that if he spoke those words he'd be unemployed within an hour, probably under observation in a mental hospital. Still, the idea was tempting. If he was fired he might stop having the dreams. And if he continued to have them after he was no longer in a position to do anything about the Cubs winning the pennant, he would know he was merely having a mental breakdown of some sort. It would be a comfort to know his troubles were on a purely human level, he thought.

Perhaps the new manager would begin having his dreams, Tiller speculated. They could compare notes, be allies, share their bewilderment.

On the other hand, Al Tiller enjoyed being the manager of a winning team. He liked the publicity. He liked being asked for his opinion. He liked having a gaggle of reporters following him about, hanging on his every word. He liked being on the cover of *Time*, even if their subheadline read, "Can a manager with the worst record in professional baseball lead the Cubbies to a pennant?"

The treadmill of dreams began early in August, in St. Louis. At first Al Tiller thought he might tell the Cubs' owner, Chester A. Rowdy. It was a thought he abandoned quickly. Four years previously, when Chester A. Rowdy bought the Cubs for thirty-seven million dollars, rumour had it that he had paid cash. He was said to have wheeled the money up to the Cub corporate offices in a Safeway basket, flanked by a Panamanian midget brandishing a machine gun. Al Tiller suspected the rumour was true, for that was the kind of man Rowdy was. Chester A. hailed from Dothan, Alabama; he hadn't learned to read or write until after he became a multimillionaire by discovering a unique worm deep in an Alabama swamp, a worm that drew fish to it the way the back of one's neck draws mosquitoes. It was said that Chester A. Rowdy was worth a hundred million by the time he was thirty.

Chester A. did not get off on the right foot with the press or the baseball fans of Chicago. The day he bought the team he announced he was going to change its name to the Chicago Worms. The Baseball Commissioner threatened to step in, but that was all he could do. Try as he might, the commissioner couldn't find any rule that said a team couldn't be called the Worms. The next week the Illinois legislature passed a law making it illegal for the Cubs to be called anything but the Cubs. Some twenty years previously the legislature had forbidden another owner to install lights in Wrigley Field.

Chester A. Rowdy baited the press. "I'm seriously considering moving the Cubs to Dothan, Alabama," he said. "I'll build me a little stadium there, seat, oh, two or three thousand. Call my team the Dothan Worms. Hell, I can afford to do it."

But he didn't. Because under his plaid suits and yellow neckties Chester A. Rowdy liked to win and liked to be seen. He was so happy back in July, the night the Cubs lengthened their lead to ten games, that he gifted Al Tiller with a red-and-white-plaid Rolls-Royce. Chester A. loved to sit in an open box at a packed Wrigley Field and be looked at. He had a bat, painted red-and-white-plaid just like his suit, and he stood up and swung it mightily when the Cubs were scoring runs, while the fans booed and cheered and the people in his box ducked like they were being shot at.

Chester A. Rowdy didn't move the team to Alabama. Instead, he bought free agents like they were jelly beans. "Hell, it's only worms," Chester A. said when he shelled out six million for the first one. Trouble was that all Chester A. knew about was worms. It soon became evident that he needed a good manager. Instead he got Al Tiller. The first year Tiller managed the Cubs, Chester A. Rowdy bought three third basemen for a few million dollars each.

When Al Tiller heard about it he called Chester A. on the telephone. "What am I supposed to do with three third basemen?" he said. "Even if they're the three best in the majors I can only play them one at a time."

"Well, hell," said Chester A., "I shouldn't have to tell you this, you're supposed to be a baseball manager, but it ain't no more than forty-five feet from third base to shortstop, and but another forty-five feet to second base; tell them fellas to adjust. For the amount I'm payin' them they better not argue about what position they get to play. Tell them that for a million dollars a year they got to adjust."

Tiller hung up and stood scratching his head. He remembered the first time Chester A. called him; he was scouting the Mexican leagues for the Minnesota Twins. "Hey, Al Tiller," a voice yelled over the static, "this here's Chester A. Rowdy. How'd you like to manage the Worms . . . I mean the Cubs?"

"Why have you chosen me?" Tiller asked. "You've got enough money to buy the best. I'm kind of a five-and-dime manager. I've never had a winning season."

"Then nobody will expect much of you, will they? If something good happens it will be a surprise. You know something, Al Tiller, I was the black sheep of a no-account family. My Pa figured some day I might steal something without gettin' caught; that was the highest expectations anybody had for me. Besides, you need the job badly enough that I figure you'll do as you're told," and he laughed.

Al Tiller's pitiful career record was not entirely his own fault. The last time he was in the majors he was 53-109 with the Texas Rangers. It was a rebuilding year; he had some pitchers who should have still been in Class A ball and a shortstop who was five years away from being an All-Star. But after a 53-109 season somebody had to go. That same team won their division four years later.

The year Tiller managed in Rookie League his team was 23-57. The team was in a town in Montana. The organization that operated the team couldn't even afford equipment. Tiller personally borrowed catching gear from the local high school. All the baseballs were brown and at least five years old. They had a kid from Arkansas with three left feet who was their designated siphoner. When they were on the road he would take a five-gallon can and a hose out to the parking lot and fill the team bus while the game was on.

"Tiller does exactly as I tell him," Chester A. Rowdy told a sportswriter once. "When I say 'Jump!' Tiller asks 'How high, Sir?' "

It hurt Al Tiller to be thought of that way by his team's owner. He knew he was not being paranoid when he said that other managers sort of sniffed when they spoke his name. "Oh, I could be with the Cubs," they said, "but only Tiller is geek enough to work for Chester A. Rowdy."

At the start of the season a sportswriter who was assessing teams for a national sports magazine wrote, "It is a unanimously acknowledged fact that Al Tiller is the dumbest manager in baseball."

Up until the Cubs, Al Tiller had never had quality players to manage. With the Cubs he chose to do unorthodox things. What did he have to lose? When Chester A. purchased the three third basemen for him, Al Tiller lined them up at the centre field wall and had them race to home plate. He made them race three times. Then he made a shortstop out of the fastest one, a second baseman out of the man who came second, while the slowest got to stay at third. He then arranged to trade the regular second baseman and shortstop in return for a good left-handed starter and a relief pitcher named Bullet Boyd who could throw aspirins and was good for two innings every night of the season.

The Cubs now had the best hitting infield in baseball. Their run production far exceeded their errors. This season they were averaging just over six runs per game, which explained why they were running away with the division.

Al Tiller had done everything but bring in a hunchback so the players could rub his hump for good luck.

Al Tiller was fifty-five years old and had twenty-seven years of coaching, scouting, and managing behind him. So if nothing else he didn't scare easily. When the dreams first came, in the dog-days of August, Al Tiller was confused but not frightened.

He was not a religious man. His mother had taken him to a couple of revival meetings when he was a kid in Oklahoma. In high school he had a girlfriend who was very devout. After she explained the whole religious scene to him he said, "You've got to be kidding. No adult who went beyond Grade 5 would believe that stuff." The girlfriend walked off in a huff, which was just as well. She married a Christian who worked in a meat packing plant, while Al Tiller became a highly unsuccessful baseball manager.

Tiller had glanced at the Gideon Bible in his hotel room perhaps only ten times in thirty years, which was one reason he found it both unnerving and confusing when biblical-looking people began crowding into his dreams.

That first time it was almost comical. The evening of the first dream it must have been 120 degrees in Busch Stadium, with the oppressive humidity making the air thick enough to cut. As he sat with his uniform melting against his skin Al Tiller remembered the story of Casey Stengel being put on the spot by a St. Louis reporter, and trying to think of something nice to say about Busch Stadium in August. After a long pause, Casey finally said, "It sure does hold the heat well."

That night after the game even the air conditioning couldn't keep the heat out of Al Tiller's hotel room. Just like when I was a kid in Oklahoma, he thought, no matter how she tried my

Ma couldn't keep the dust out of the house; it seeped through the siding, the ceiling, right through the glass in the windows.

He blamed the first dream on the heat. In his dream he was seated in a balcony of some sort, looking down; it might have been an operating theatre, there was so much white light flooding it. There didn't appear to be walls, just curtains of light, white as satin in some places, translucent as ice in others. Behind a desk, topped with what could have been white marble, sat an old man. He had white hair and a beard. His face was set in a severe expression. His clothing was right out of the Old Testament, flowing robes of ice-blue lined with material of a flamingo-pink colour. His hands were clasped in front of him on the desk top, his nails were large and square. He should be carrying a staff, Al Tiller thought, but couldn't see one anywhere.

Across the desk from the old man, seated in a semi-circle, were five people, ordinary looking, dressed in pale, twentieth-century clothing. Each sat on a polished wooden chair with claw-feet; the seat of each chair was upholstered in expensive-looking ice-blue velvet.

"Please, God," the man furthest away from Tiller was saying, "we'd like you to arrange for the Chicago Cubs to win the pennant this year."

Nightmares like that are brought on by too much pizza, too many beers; the pressure getting to a frazzled baseball manager, Al Tiller thought, as he recalled the event the next day. He was embarrassed by the mundane quality of the dreams: the scenes were so archetypal, the characters such stock dream-characters. Apparently I can't even dream with imagination, he thought.

The five people gathered around God were, Al Tiller discovered, representative of baseball fans, how many he wasn't able to determine, but certainly a large contingent, all apparently deceased. Lobbying, Tiller supposed, was the word for what they were doing. Each one, in turn, pleaded politely with God to see that the Chicago Cubs won the pennant.

He woke in the dark, in that clammy hotel room in St. Louis, his heart thumping like a bongo drum, his breath coming in short gasps. It was 4:00 a.m. He got up, dressed, went down to the lobby, and sat in one of the deep sofas until the coffee shop opened. By then he had decided it was just a nightmare; he even mentioned the experience casually to his pitching coach, when the coach joined him for breakfast.

"We need all the help we can get," the coach said. "If you get to put in a word, ask for some complete games from our starting pitchers."

That evening the Cubs got nine innings of four-hit pitching from a player who hadn't gone more than six innings all year.

Later that night Al Tiller dreamed again. The scene was the same, only the petitioners were different. He never mentioned his nocturnal experiences to anyone again.

The dreams continued. It embarrassed Tiller somewhat to see all the men pleading, "Please, God." They weren't all men either; there was usually one woman in each group. On the third night a small woman, in a flowered dress that looked like it was made from a bedsheet, was very adamant. "It's time for the Chicago Cubs to win their division," she said.

"And the National League pennant," said a runty guy with a big nose, who looked like someone he should know, Al Tiller thought.

"And the World Series," said a hefty, white-haired man who, Tiller decided, was Richard Daley, the man who was mayor of Chicago, almost forever, back in the '60s and '70s.

"We're not greedy, God," said the runty guy. "Just help the Cubs win the National League pennant; we'll take our chances on the World Series."

"We'd like it to happen this year," said the woman, "when the National League team is home for the World Series. We'd rather not have the Cubs in a series where there is a designated hitter."

Tiller had the feeling that "this year" might have been two, or four, or six years ago. Who knows, he thought, maybe they have video tape. In fact, when he woke he often pictured himself, his face like a tape deck, a cartridge being plunged into his open mouth. It was like the dreams were cluing him in, gradually, to a situation that had been building for a number of years, perhaps all the way back to the last time the Cubs won a pennant, an ongoing procedure, building pressure, gaining followers, trying to convince God to let the Cubs win a pennant.

Al Tiller dreamed for six nights: in St. Louis, in Cincinnati, and finally, back in Chicago. On the seventh night he slept deeply and without dreams. The cycle then started again. For all six nights the scenes were much the same: a conference table, God at the head, white light, each time a different assortment of people begging. Some were polite, some were demanding. Tiller was certain Frank Chance was there, and Three Finger Brown, and Frankie Frisch. On the fifth night Joe Tinker was there wearing his Cub uniform.

It struck Al Tiller that all he heard was pleading, whining, outright requests. He supposed that was what God must have come to expect. To Al Tiller prayers had always seemed to be an extremely self-centred pastime.

As the seriousness of the situation became clear to him he was tempted to surrender his honour, to work toward losing rather than winning. He knew it was much easier than people imagined for a manager to influence the outcome of a baseball game.

We're ahead 4-2, last of the eighth, he thought. Eddie Guest, my ace pitcher, is tiring, doing all the things only an expert can spot: dropping his right shoulder an inch or more than normal, bending his left knee too little. How long should I leave him in? He walks the first batter, a bad sign. I slump out to the mound hitching up my pants. "How's he doing?" I ask the catcher. Never trust a pitcher. They'll swear on their mother's grave they've still got stuff, even after they've given up ten straight hits. "His curve's not breakin', otherwise okay," says the catcher. "Stay away from the curve," I tell Eddie, slap his shoulder, and head back for the dugout. Next batter lays down a perfect bunt. Men on first and second. My instinct tells me that if we want to win now is the time to change pitchers. But if I want to help the team lose, I leave him in. No one will fault me for letting him pitch to one more batter. The next guy drives the ball off the scoreboard and waltzes into third standing up. Score tied. I bring in Bullet Boyd. The man on third scores on a sacrifice fly. We're down 4-5. We lose. I did it.

It was on the sixth night God spoke. Tiller was certain that Al Capone was one of the lobbyists that evening. He had always thought of Capone as a White Sox fan.

God cleared his throat before he spoke; his voice sounded as if it were emanating from an echo chamber. My dreams are like "B" movies, or bad television, Al Tiller thought. I couldn't let anyone know about them without apologizing for their quality. When God did speak he sounded to Al Tiller a little like a senator.

"I appreciate your interest," God said. "I want to assure you that I hold the Chicago Cubs in highest esteem. I have listened to your entreaties and considered the matter carefully from all angles. I am aware of how long it has been since the Cubs have won a pennant. I think you should know that when the Cubs next win the National League Championship, it will be the last pennant before Armageddon. . . ."

Al Tiller assumed that there was more, however that was the point at which he woke up, his sweat-soaked pyjamas wrapped around him like wet sheets, his heart thrumming. His last sight had been of the lobbyists leaping to their feet with joy as if their favourite player had just homered in a clutch situation. Had God added something that Al Tiller hadn't heard? Had he granted the request?

"The last pennant before Armageddon!" The words danced before Al Tiller's eyes; they were there in the mirror when he stared at his aging face the next morning; they had been suspended in the clouds when the first pinkness of dawn oozed over the horizon.

He was on the steps of the Chicago Public Library when it opened. He looked up "Armageddon" in every dictionary and biblical reference book available; he studied a biblical concordance and tracked down every reference in the Scriptures.

The last struggle of the forces of good and evil against each other. A clash of God's truth opposed to Satan's error. To take place on Judgement Day. The end of the world as we know it.

The end of the world, Al Tiller thought. When my Cubs next win a pennant, which could be only weeks away, the world will end soon after, and I'm the only one who knows about it.

That was when he remembered the archangel. I am not alone, he thought. There is a radio talk-show host in St. Louis and his audience, all of whom know. And that's when he realized that his affliction had started not with the dreams, but back in June.

After the game that June evening, which Chicago lost 4-2, Al Tiller went back to his hotel and turned on the radio to a phone-in show called *Talking Baseball*. It was one of those shows where fans called in and made comments on baseball in general and the St. Louis Cardinals in particular. Not a very exciting show: one fan wanted to know why the Cards didn't play one of their second-stringers more often. The host pointed out that the player in question had a .221 average and couldn't field a basketball. Tiller pricked up his ears when a woman caller claimed to be the granddaughter of old-time Cubs' pitcher Zip Zabel, who pitched from 1913 to 1915. The call didn't last long; the host didn't have much to say to Zip Zabel's granddaughter.

The next caller caught everyone's interest.

"I am an archangel," he said.

"That's very interesting," said the host, "has this anything to do with baseball?"

"I am a blind archangel," the caller replied.

"Perhaps you should be calling the Interfaith Network. Father Silas emcees the call-in show over there. I could give you the number."

"I wish to make a prophecy," said the archangel.

"To do with baseball?"

"The Chicago Cubs will win the last pennant before Armageddon."

"That's very interesting. Is that all?"

"I mean it to be taken seriously. It *is* a prophecy," said the archangel.

"The Chicago Cubs will win the last pennant before Armageddon?'' repeated the host.

"That's correct."

"You should be telling Al Tiller, that will be the best news he's had in years." There was about five seconds of dead air. "On the other hand, this Armageddon business sounds pretty serious."

"Indeed it is," said the archangel.

"You wouldn't care to tell us your name; I mean your archangel name. Could we look you up in the Scriptures?''

"The prophecy speaks for itself."

"Ah, well, thank you for calling."

"My pleasure," said the archangel.

"It certainly takes all kinds," said the host, switching to another line.

On September 28th the Cubs clinched the National League Eastern Division Championship. In the clubhouse the jubilant players doused Al Tiller with champagne. He found it very sticky and it smarted like hell when it got in his eyes. He tried to act the part of the celebrant. He slapped a few backs and shook a lot of hands. He let the press photograph him, barechested, hoisting the trophy above his head, the bullpen catcher standing on a chair behind him, frothing champagne onto his hair.

The Cubs were now to meet the Dodgers in the playoff for the National League pennant. Tiller had considered the possibility of aiding his team to lose the division, but he passed up every opportunity presented him. While the Cubs did indeed play less than .500 baseball during the stretch Tiller was managing to the best of his ability. Once, with a six-run lead, Al Tiller left his dead-tired pitcher in the game when he knew in his heart he should have brought in a reliever. As he sat in the dugout, his hands trembling, he looked around like a shoplifter trying to spot a store detective, sure that every player and fan in the ballpark had him spotted for a fraud. But as he watched, his pitcher reached back and found something extra; he fanned the side in the ninth and made Tiller look like a genius.

What if we *are* getting supernatural help? thought Al Tiller.

If we are, then why am I having these dreams? Who wants me to know what's going on? Am I just a lonely old manager having nightmares?

Still, each time an opponent's line-drive curved into foul territory, or an extra-base hit found its way into one of his outfielder's gloves, or when an opposing pitcher stood trance-like on the mound instead of covering first base, Al Tiller wondered.

At the library, Al Tiller read that the armour of God for the battle of Armageddon was said to be Truth, Righteousness, Peace, Faith, Salvation, and the Spirit. He did not exactly understand the paradox of peace in war, or what exactly the Spirit was. He wondered where honour fit in. He had always considered himself an honourable man. Honour was *his* armour. He had always tried to cause as little pain as possible. He treated his players as he would like to be treated. In spite of his attitude, most of his players held him in mild contempt, the remainder were indifferent. The lowest paid player on his club made more money than he did.

Grizzled was the adjective sportswriters most often used when describing Al Tiller. He guessed it was accurate. He was surprised at the age in his eyes as he stared out from the covers of *Time* and *Sports Illustrated*. His hair was an off-white, his eyebrows craggy, and his face looked as though an artist had drawn in the deep tension lines between his brows, and the heavy seams which ran down from the corners of his mouth. The veins on the backs of his hands were dark blue and the size of pencils.

Tiller tried his best to be nice to sportswriters, always had; he tried to come up with interesting quotes, never held back information. But even after winning the division, after entering the pennant playoff as favourites, the press were still inordinately interested in the fact that Tiller had the worst won-lost record of any manager in professional baseball. He often wondered what they expected of him. Managers who threw tantrums and punches and locked the clubhouse door to the press got more respect. He accepted that if the Cubs lost the pennant Chester A. Rowdy would probably take back the red-and-white-plaid Rolls-Royce, and he would probably let him.

Even his nickname, "the Hun," was kind of a joke, nothing to do with prowess or skill. The year he managed Spokane in the Pacific Coast League his team started the season 1-16 and for the seventeenth loss committed an error an inning. Al Tiller didn't get hostile very often, but after that game he really chewed out his team. When the players came out of the locker-room there was one cub reporter still lurking under the stands. "Was he mad?" he asked a big first baseman, who now taught English at a community college in Wyoming. "He behaved like a regular Al Tiller the Hun," replied the first baseman.

Al Tiller had more to worry about than the dreams that invaded his body six nights out of seven. After the Cubs clinched the division championship and waited for the season to end and the playoffs to begin, the world situation took a marked turn for the worse. Al Tiller read the newspaper and magazine accounts with a deepening interest. He had scant knowledge of the international situation; all he knew was that Sri Lanka, a small island in the Indian Ocean, had suddenly become a trouble-spot, the spot where World War Three appeared ready to start. The Russians had troops in Sri Lanka, the Americans said they shouldn't be there. The Americans threatened to remove the Russian troops by force. Both sides were making war-like sounds.

It would certainly be fitting, thought Al Tiller, that if there *were* supernatural powers they would be capricious enough to stake the end of the world on the outcome of a best-of-five baseball series.

Tiller pored over the biblical prophesies concerning Armageddon. They remained as much a mystery as when he first encountered them. What he desired most of all was a dreamless sleep.

Tiller had read that a respect for one's word was a wealth not to be squandered. That's the only kind of wealth I've ever acquired, he thought; in fact, the value he placed on honour and duty had radically changed his life.

Nearly thirty-five years before, Al Tiller played a mediocre second base for a team in Little Rock, Arkansas, in an almost forgotten minor league. One thing that tickled him was that sportswriters hadn't dug back that far; if they had they would have found that he never enjoyed a winning season as a player either. That year Al Tiller was considered a player to watch. Management figured his bat would come around with seasoning. It never did. He never batted higher than .236 in his career.

After the home-opener in Little Rock, there was a public reception for the team and there Al Tiller met the mayor's daughter. She had shoulder-length black hair, ebony eyes, and skin the colour of polished maple. She wore an ivory-coloured sheath-dress and a corsage of pink flowers of a kind more exotic than Al Tiller had ever seen in Oklahoma. She was vivacious, funny, and, compared to Al Tiller, worldly. The mayor had business interests in New York, Boston, Chicago; she had seen more major-league games than Al had. He fell in love with her. He thought she was in love with him too, although he knew half the young men in Little Rock were in love with her that summer.

She could tease life into him. Al Tiller had never felt so alive. He was enchanted with the lushness of the South after the hot sand and scorpions of Oklahoma. She was like one of the strange, fragrant blooms that seemed to grow so casually in the South. He remembered her standing on her tiptoes to kiss him, her fingers cool on the back of his neck. For Al Tiller it was very important to have someone to care for, someone to show off for. He knew that with her beside him he could reach back for the extra resources, grit his teeth, narrow his eyes, and become a great baseball player.

But that fall she suddenly announced she was going off to a university in Connecticut. "I need my freedom," she said. Al Tiller couldn't have been more stunned if she'd cracked him across the teeth with a baseball bat. He knew he should follow her. In fact her father advised him to. But he didn't. Al Tiller always tried to have respect for other people's feelings. If she wants to be free, who am I to stand in her way, he thought. In December she married a Harvard Law School senior.

The mayor phoned Al Tiller at home in Oklahoma.

"I wish it had been you, Al," he said. "This boy's credentials are impeccable, but damn, Al, it's just like parking another silver Cadillac in the driveway. He's got no personality. And he races funny little boats; and he has nerve enough to call what he does a sport."

"I'm hurtin' too," said Al. "At least she's still your daughter."

Al played in Little Rock the next summer, while his teammates from the previous year were now in Triple A, edging their way toward the majors.

Back in his home town of Zane Grey, Oklahoma, he started dating a girl he had grown up with.

His third summer in Little Rock was a make-it-or-break-it season. His hitting had to improve. In the spring before he left for Little Rock, he became engaged; the wedding was set for November.

In June he received a call from the mayor's daughter. Her marriage had failed and she was returning to Little Rock. Would he see her?

When they met, Al Tiller found that nothing had changed. He trembled as he took her cool hands in his and leaned close to kiss her cheek. He was as much in love with her as he had ever been.

Now he had a choice to make. In a way he loved the girl he was engaged to; although they held no surprises for each other, she was warm, tender, and innocent. But to go back on his promise to her wouldn't be honourable.

When he thought of his first love he ached with passion. Still there was really no choice at all. For Al Tiller honour was all important.

He made one rather curt phone call.

The marriage took place as scheduled. The girl from Zane Grey, Oklahoma, was a very good wife to him. They had three lovely daughters and almost thirty years together. Yet Al Tiller often wondered what his life would have been like if he had done what he truly wanted to do rather than let his sense of honour prevail.

His first love, the mayor's daughter — even now he couldn't bring himself to use her name — died of leukemia at thirty. He often wondered just how different his life would have been if he had lived those precious years with her.

Matters of honour survive everything, Al Tiller thought. He was now faced with another impossible decision.

He wished he could be certain of what was really happening. It was possible, he thought, that he was simply an old and unsuccessful baseball manager cracking under the strain of a long season. He wished he wasn't so alone.

In St. Louis for the final games of the season he phoned the radio talk-show host, the man who had taken the call from the archangel.

"This is Al Tiller," he said, lowering his voice; *an endearing growl* was how sportswriters described his voice.

"I'm honoured," said the host. "What can I do for you?"

"I'll be happy to go on the air later, answer questions from fans and all that, but first I'd like to discuss something privately."

"Shoot," said the host.

"You remember the archangel?" Tiller said. "The guy who predicted the Cubs would win the last pennant before Armageddon? Well, I was wondering what you thought of his prediction in light of the present world conditions and all? Frankly, I'm a little worried."

"I'm afraid I don't understand, Mr Tiller," said the host, hesitating. "What archangel? What prediction?"

"I guess I must be mistaken," Tiller said, with as much joviality as he could muster. "It's not important anyway."

Had the phone-in show been a dream too? Al Tiller asked himself. Did I really come back to my hotel from Busch Stadium and fall asleep on my bed?

The first two games of the pennant playoff were held at Wrigley Field in perfect, sunny, October weather. The sportswriters made a lot of jokes about the sun shining on Al Tiller and the Cubs. His ace, Eddie Guest, pitched a four-hitter in the opener and the Cubs scored eleven runs. Chicago scored six runs in the first inning of the second game on the way to an easy 9-2 win.

When the series shifted to Chavez Ravine in Los Angeles, the Dodgers bombed the Cubs 8-1 and 10-3 to even the series.

Neither Tiller nor the Dodger manager had anything to do in the way of managing. It had been a hitter's series.

After the Cubs won the Eastern Division championship they were given a ticker-tape parade. The mayor presented Al Tiller with a key to the city of Chicago. A pennant would be the gold at the end of the rainbow for Al Tiller. He was sick with longing for it. He was also terrified of it. After the parade there were fireworks: blue, red, and green stars exploding over Lake Michigan. To Tiller they weren't joyous; they spelled out Armageddon.

The six scenes in Al Tiller's dreams were always the same, like six tapes, played and replayed. The evening before the final game had been a sixth night. More than anything else Al Tiller wished for a dreamless sleep. He considered trying to drown the apparitions with whiskey, rejected the idea; rejected asking the team physician for a sedative.

Tense as piano wire he waited for sleep, trying to make his mind clear and blank. But when sleep came the dream came with it, silvery as moonlight, like a tiny tornado of stardust floating in through the glass of the window and burrowing into Al Tiller's sleeping form. He knew immediately the dream was subtly changed, but it took him a few seconds to recognize how. The woman in the group of supplicants, though her back was turned, was not a stranger. Tiller's heart dropped, his stomach rose until the two collided. His blood careened through his body until his eyes seemed glazed by a red haze. When she spoke he recognized the voice of his first love, and no angelic choir could have sounded sweeter. "Please, God," she said, "I would like the Chicago Cubs to win the pennant this year," and as she spoke she turned her chair and stared directly at Al Tiller, her lips slightly parted, her eyes as full of love as the day he had last been with her.

A pennant. Armageddon. Another chance, Al Tiller thought. Now I have the most important reason of all to manage to win, something beyond honour, beyond duty. For surely, when all is said and done, love is more important.

After eight innings the final game was tied 2-2. A pitcher's duel. Al Tiller had had no serious decisions to make.

Even as they played the world situation continued to deteriorate. In the dugout several of the players had portable radios pressed to their ears. American ships travelling full-out toward Sri Lanka were due to arrive momentarily. "It is our duty to liberate the island," said the president of the United States.

The Soviet president said the moment an American foot or an American bomb landed on Sri Lanka the U.S.S.R. would retaliate in the most severe manner imaginable.

"We are not afraid," the president of the United States told the people.

In the bottom of the ninth Eddie Guest got the first two men out; he then walked two batters, both after long battles: the first had fouled off ten pitches, the second twelve.

The telltale signs were all there: Eddie was dropping his right shoulder too much, bending his left knee too little. Bullet Boyd was well rested, more than ready. Al Tiller shuffled out to the mound.

"How's he doin'?" he asked the catcher.

"Everything but the curveball," the catcher replied. "He shoulda struck out them last two guys. They was lucky."

Al Tiller kicked the dirt. He thought of the American Navy perhaps putting down a beachhead at that very moment. He wondered what the honourable thing was to do? He wondered about duty. He ached with love.

"Don't throw the curve," he said to Eddie Guest, and patted his shoulder. In the bullpen he saw Bullet Boyd throw his glove to the ground.

Then, honour intact, Al Tiller slouched toward the dugout, prepared to suffer.

The Baseball Spur

The Baseball Spur

For Tony

1.

"Walt (No Neck) Williams, do you remember him?" Stan asks suddenly, in the way he has of jumping from subject to subject.

"Um-hmm," I say noncommittally, after racking my brain for a few seconds. "I know the name but the details are fuzzy."

"He played for the Sox. The White Sox. They called him No Neck because he didn't have one," and Stan laughs his long, stuttering laugh, sounding as though he has peanut shells lodged in his throat. There is a car following us closely and the headlights bury themselves in the rear-view mirror, which paints a moonlight-like bar across Stan's face. As I glance sideways it looks as though he is wearing a golden mask.

"Last summer I met No Neck on the street in Chicago," Stan goes on. "I just about went crazy. 'Hey, No Neck,' I called to him, and I set down my suitcase and went running

after him. You remember that, Gloria?'' he directs the last
words to his wife, turning toward the back seat to acknowledge
her, the mask slipping around over his ear as he does. Gloria is
a big, blowzy, Polish girl, cheerful and resilient. She has fouled
off all the curves life has thrown at her, although over the years
her brows have squeezed together in a mini-scowl as if she had
been staring too long at the horizon.

"He actually edged away from me. You remember that,
Gloria? I guess you must meet a lot of nuts when you're in the
Bigs. I mean I kept saying to him, 'Man, I used to watch you
when you played for the Sox. You were great, man. You were
great.' And I hauled out my wallet and looked for something he
could sign, and I didn't have any paper, not even a Master
Charge slip or anything, so I got him to sign the back of
Gloria's picture. It's one I've carried around for ten years,
with Gloria in jeans and her hair up in a bee-hive standing
beside her old man's '69 Buick. No Neck looked at me like I
was crazy, leaving my wife with our suitcases and chasing after
him for a block like that. Don't you remember him, Jackie?''

"I know the name, but I don't get involved with modern-
day players the way you do, Stan," I say. My own wife,
Sunny, is squashed into the corner of the back seat behind me.
She hasn't said a word since we left the ballpark in Cedar
Rapids. I catch a glimpse of the red glow of her cigarette. She is
tiny as a child sitting back there. I wonder how someone so
small and insignificant-looking can tear me apart the way she
does.

"No Neck's only a couple of years older than us, Jackie,"
Stan says. "Played his last game in '75. God, you know how
that makes me feel. A guy just two years older than me retired.
And me still strugglin' to make the Bigs.''

"You'll make it, Stan," I say automatically, just as I have
been saying it every year for over half my life.

Stan and Gloria have come to visit Gloria's mother in
Onamata; she's the only family either of them have here
anymore. Stan's father is dead and his mother has gone to
Florida to live with a married sister.

Since spring Stan has been playing Triple A ball in San Antonio, but he sprained his right hand pretty badly a couple of weeks ago and the club put him on the disabled list and brought up a kid from a Class C team in Burlington to replace him.

"I wanted to ask No Neck about how much he practised. I bet he practised like crazy or he never would have got to the Bigs. God, but I used to practise. Remember how I used to practise, Jackie, Gloria? Hey, Sunny, you're being awful quiet. I ever told you how I practised?"

Sunny draws deeply on her cigarette, but does not answer. Stan is tall and muscular, his head square, his hair cut short, but his face as wide and innocent as a husky child's. His eyes are pale blue and wide-set, his hair, though it's darker now, was a lemony colour when we were kids, and Stan was forever watering it as if it were grass that would grow stronger if wet.

"My old man never liked baseball, but I used to make him come outside and he'd stand in front of the barn and I'd make him hit fly balls to me. I spent all my pay on baseballs, all the money I earned working for old Piska the cement contractor. Saturdays I used to carry a bucket of cement in each hand from the mortar box to the sidewalk we were laying, or the garage floor. I took the money and I bought a box of baseballs, a whole dozen. I laid them out on my bed like a bagful of white oranges, and I smelled them, and touched them, and handled them like a miser fondling his money. The old man wasn't very good and every once in a while he'd foul one into the goddamn pig pen. I'd have to wash the pigshit off it, and sometimes when I went in the pen one of those big red buggers would have the ball in his teeth, and I'd have to whack his snout to make him let go and the ball would have teeth marks on it forever." Stan stops for a second or two. The highway is dark. There is an orangy flash behind me as Sunny lights a new cigarette. I see her left eye is closed, squinted up against the smoke. There is an inch-long scar, pink as a worm on her dusky skin, running vertically from the corner of her eye onto her cheekbone. There are fine age lines spreading out from the corners of her eyes. Sunny aged a good deal the last time she was away.

"I love the game. I've always loved the game, right Jackie? I used to dream about a career in baseball. It wasn't just vague hopes like a lot of kids have. I knew what I was doing. I've made a living from the game for almost fifteen years. And I'm gonna make the Bigs yet, you wait and see.''

"You'll make it, Stan. We all know that," I say.

"I mean I've seen guys with twice as much talent as me throw it all away. They party all night and stagger in ten minutes before a game wearing their hangovers like badges. It's not fair that my reflexes are a hundredth of a second slower than theirs. I mean I work out three hours every afternoon. I've always hustled, haven't I Jackie?''

"You've always hustled," says Gloria from the darkness. Her voice is lifeless. She answers by rote. We've both learned to agree with Stan without even listening to him.

"I put a washtub on its side, used it for homeplate, and I'd make the catch and rear back, and I got so I could hit that tub on the first or second bounce about nine times out of ten. You know what the difference is between the Bigs and the minors?'' Stan waits only one beat, not expecting an answer. "Consistency. The whole thing is consistency. There are players in the minors who make spectacular plays and hit the ball just as hard as in the majors, but the guys in the Bigs are more consistent. They make the plays not just nine out of ten times but ninety-nine times out of a hundred." He pauses thoughtfully for a moment. "You know, I'd hit nine out of ten, but that other one might end up thirty feet down the line, or hit the barn door fifteen feet in the air, making a sound like a gun going off. Hey, Jackie, how about you come out and hit me some flies in the morning?''

2.

When we got home after the game I kissed Sunny gently and pulled her against me. Her lips were dry and she made them thin and did not return my kiss. I did everything I could think of to please her. I touched her with my fingertips, gently undressed her, massaged her, fondled her, loved her with my hands, my tongue, held back my own passion, waited for a response from her, received none.

I remember once, at a time like this, when Sunny was in one of her moods, she said something bitter, something designed to make me hate her.

"Can't you tell by the way I touch you that I love you?" I said.

"No," said Sunny, precipitating a long silence.

Eventually I made love with her. Actually I made love to her, not with her. Her body was unpliant, mannequin-like. I wanted so desperately to arouse her, I controlled myself carefully, rocked her so gently for a long time until our bodies were slick and delicious.

"Can't you finish up," Sunny said, not even in a whisper. "I'm tired."

If she knew how close I came to killing her it would have made her happy.

I threw myself off her without a word and lay like a rock in the darkness, my body taut, nerve ends twitching. Late in the night I heard her leave. I woke to the tinkling of hangers in our closet, knew she was packing a few blouses, a couple of pairs of jeans in the same battered black suitcase she arrived with twelve years ago. I lay, tense as piano wire, afraid to speak, afraid not to. She closed the front door quietly; I listened to her tiny footsteps descend the stairs, fade away as she moved down the sidewalk. Where does she go? How does she get there? There are no buses, no traffic. I suppose she walks to the interstate, stands at the side of the road . . . I can hear the sinister hiss of air-brakes as a truck pulls over.

I recall a night many years ago, when I ran out of a restaurant after her, frantic that I might never see her again. I recall the face of a man in a Tennessee pick-up truck. I don't suppose he was over thirty-five, although he looked old to me. I'll never forget the uncomprehending look of loss and pain on his face. I've seen that look many times since. My reflection wears it like a tragic mask.

3.

I met Sunny twelve years ago, at the restaurant in Iowa City were I worked part-time. She came in accompanied by a large rumpled-looking man who was dressed in a blue pin-stripe suit. He was tall and cadaverous and it was impossible to guess their relationship. He might have been father, husband, lover, brother. As they crossed the dining room she trailed after him, a waif covered in a feathery-grey calf-length dress of some material that seemed to attach itself to her, as if both she and the cloth were charged with static electricity.

Her chest was flat, her dark hair hacked in a boyish cut; her lips were thin and when she did open her mouth there were spaces between each of her teeth. She took a crumpled pack of Winston's from a very used-looking handbag that had once been black leather. The man ignored her as she searched the tiny purse until she found a book of matches. She squinted her left eye to keep the smoke at bay, drew deeply on the cigarette, licked her lower lip with a cat-pink tongue.

By the time I approached their table to ask if I could get them anything from the bar, I was in love. Sunny was hunched over the table smoking as if she expected to be arrested for it. Her eyes were brilliant, the irises an orchid-violet, floating in whites pure as snow. I tried to imagine my tongue bringing her tiny nipples erect. I wanted to taste her mouth, feel her tongue exploring my teeth. She might have been fifteen; she might have been thirty. It didn't matter.

All through the meal I circled their table like a hawk, replenishing their water, coffee, lighting Sunny's cigarettes, asking again and again if the meal was satisfactory. The man had a deep voice with a strong southern accent; Sunny's voice was breathy in a peculiar sort of way, as if she were acting, speaking in a voice not entirely her own. They talked very little. I eavesdropped on every word, ignoring my other tables. In spite of my attentiveness I was unable to learn her name, their business, or their relationship.

In desperation I followed them to the parking lot as they left the restaurant, tearing off my apron, grabbing my jacket from the pronged chrome hanger next to the bar. They got in a faded red pick-up truck with Tennessee licence plates. I memorized the number — in fact I still remember it, PNT-791 — and I stood helplessly as they pulled away, envisioning myself writing to Motor Vehicle Registration in Nashville to obtain a name and an address. To my immense relief the truck simply pulled across the street and stopped in the parking lot of the Evangelical Christian Church. The man got out, lumbered toward a side door, and disappeared inside.

As I walked up to the passenger side of the truck Sunny glanced at me. I motioned for her to roll down the window, which she did.

"You're very beautiful," I said.

She looked at me, really looked at me for the first time; I prayed she'd like what she saw. She smiled then and I could tell it was involuntary. I bet I'm the first person who's ever told her she's beautiful, I thought. And she was, to me, in that magic way no one can explain. Her nose was too flat, and her hair looked like she cut it herself to spite someone. She was covered in freckles, even her fingers were freckled. And I smiled at her as if I were witnessing a miracle, and recalled how, when she brushed past me as she entered the restaurant, I got the first whiff of her, a tangy sweetness, not of perfume but of *her*. And I could feel my tongue rearranging the freckles on her neck, her breasts, her belly. And the feeling has never left me, will never leave me; the breathlessness, the tightness in my chest when Sunny enters a room. The desire that makes my knees weak. The love that makes me able to endure the way she tortures me.

Sunny is one of those women who comes and goes. Whatever demons she wrestles with require that she be on the move a good part of her life. She vanishes for days, weeks, months, then returns as mysteriously as she leaves. It is like she is alternately plucked from my life, and parachuted back into it.

4.

She eventually climbed down out of the truck. Reaching over
the tail-gate she heaved out a small, black, overnight bag. We
stood talking for a while. I babbled nervously about my job,
about the big old house, ten miles away in Onamata, where I
lived alone, about my interest in baseball history. I told her of
my plan to do a master's thesis on the history of the Iowa Baseball Confederacy, a semi-pro league that existed in Eastern
Iowa shortly after the turn of the century. I didn't realize at the
time that she told me nothing.

"Can I buy you a drink?" I finally said, waving vaguely
toward the restaurant, toward the rest of the town. "That is if
you're old enough to . . ."

"I'm old enough to do anything," said Sunny. And I think,
under her breath, she added, "And I have." But I was never
sure.

Just as we were leaving the truck, the side door of the church
opened and the truck-owner stepped outside. I didn't know
what was expected of me. Sunny seemed willing to continue
right on. I stopped, turned my head in the direction of the
man, who held-up suddenly, making a skidding sound on the
gravel.

Sunny turned and waved, a cheery, impersonal gesture.
"Thanks for the ride," she said, "maybe I'll see you around."

The man raised a hand, not waving but a gesture as if he
were reaching out for her. Then he joined his two large, help-
less hands together at belt-level. He didn't speak but his
gesture and his stricken face said more than he intended. We
continued across the street and toward downtown. Sunny
never looked back; I glanced over my shoulder once, the man
was standing in the same position.

"There's an old bar called Donnelly's," I said. "Dark wood
and dark mirrors, you'll like it."

"First thing I want is to hit the john and get rid of this,"
Sunny said, running her hands down the slippery, clinging
material of her dress. "This was his idea, said it makes me look
Amish or something."

5.

I shouldn't allow her to come back each time as if nothing has happened. I should be angry. I should curse and scream and punish. Each time I am alone I promise myself I won't take her back. If I do there will be conditions, perhaps even written down, a contract.

But then a car stops on the gravel deep in the night. A door slams. There is a long silence. I picture her standing, small as a child in the darkness, psyching herself up for what she is about to do. Then comes the crunch of her small steps on the gravel; the door opens. Silence while her eyes get used to the dark.

At the bedroom door: "Jack?" She is smoking a cigarette.

"Over here." She bumps a table, finds the ashtray on it. I always keep one there, although I have never smoked. There is a tiny crackling as she puts out her cigarette. She takes off her jacket and tosses it on the floor. Her arms go up in a supple motion and her tee-shirt skids over her head. She kicks one boot off with the help of the other, bends and dispatches the second one. My desire for her is so wild I feel as if I'm all liquid. I can smell her; the tart, sweet scent of her sweat. The odour of a car interior. I grab the waist of her jeans, pull her toward me until she stands at the edge of the bed. Her nipples are like hard candy. The musky, smokey taste of her fills my senses. Her mouth finds mine. Her tongue is like a bird set free. She tastes faintly of whiskey.

"Fantasy Land," I say, tossing back the covers, pulling her down on top of me.

6.

There was never any question about her coming home with me that first night. We sat in Donnelly's for a while. I talked, Sunny studied me, eyeing me as if she were figuring some kind of odds, trying to guess how I would react to her secrets. She pursed her lips each time she laughed, making laughter seem a gesture of self-control.

At the bar, Sunny fished her clothes from her small bag, disappeared to the washroom, emerged in jeans, a white blouse, a tattered denim jacket faded to the colour of skim milk. She returned from the washroom empty-handed, the dress nowhere to be seen, "I have more lives than a cat," she said in reply to my questioning look. "I just used one of them up."

"You'll need a dress to get married in," I said.

"You mean that, don't you?" she said, crinkling her nose, her violet eyes measuring me again.

"I mean it," I said.

"Then you'll have to buy me another one."

Later, as I stopped the car in front of my home, I turned to Sunny where she sat, her thigh touching mine. "You wear your clothes as though you want to be helped out of them," I whispered, my fingers unbuttoning a button on her blouse. Suddenly, Sunny grabbed onto me fiercely, her mouth melting into mine. She held me as if her life depended on getting closer to me than anyone had ever been.

My passion was so complete it was more than enough for both of us. She loved the house; my tall, square, white-painted house. Sixty years old, its green shutters the colour of spring leaves, solid, permanent, an anchor, a rock, a root. Sunny explored it the next morning, tentatively, poking her head into each room before allowing her body to follow. The floors of the bedrooms and living room were a sunshine yellow; the rooms smelled subtly of wax, of dust, of old upholstery.

"Do you like it?" I asked.

"It's like a fairy tale. You're sure it's yours?"

"It can be yours too. I need to share this with someone." I put my arm tightly around her waist.

"This is really yours? I mean, I've dreamed of a big, solid home like this. If I drew a picture of the house I've dreamed about this would be it. And it's really yours? You're so young. Your parents aren't coming home next week from somewhere?"

"My father's dead. I have a mother in Chicago, who's married to a very rich man. And a sister who blows up buildings."

"Really?"

"Everyone should have an outlaw for a sister," I said.

7.

I've always felt that Sunny's biggest quarrel with me is that I haven't treated her as badly as she thinks I should.

"I'm trouble," she said in the sweet darkness of my bedroom. "Don't say I didn't warn you."

"I'm warned," I said.

"I'm a little like smoke," Sunny said. "There isn't a door I can't get under, or over, or through, or around."

"I'll take my chances," I said.

8.

For two years, while Sunny was gone, I even tried dating. I hung around the University of Iowa Bookstore, a bar called the Airliner that was frequented by students, a restaurant known as Bushnell's Turtle. But the girls I met, just as they were ten years before, were either too young, too silly, or too serious. I hate dewy-eyed girls talking about meaningful relationships; I hate perfumes, deodorants, hair-sprays, sweaters and bras and knitted dresses, manicured nails, cosmetics, loud music, football pennants, stuffed animals, and vegetarian dishes. Each one I met was so eager and so inexperienced. I talked a lot about Sunny.

9.

"I've done things that would curl your hair," Sunny said to me once in the warmth of our bed. She had just returned from a two-month absence.

"Don't tantalize me," I said fiercely. "If you want to tell me, tell me. If you don't, shut up. There's nothing you can tell me that will change how I feel about you."

"Maybe I should try?"

"Sunny, whatever it is you want, I won't do it. I won't punish you. I won't abandon you. I won't send you away. I refuse to cage you. You have to stay with me because you love me."

10.

I didn't fully realize it, until I stood staring into the half-empty closet the morning after Sunny left me for the first time, but my mother was another one of those women who come and go. I suddenly remembered my father rambling through empty rooms of this same house, stopping to stare into the same half-empty closet, shaking his head in disbelief, then going into his study and staying there for days. It is the same study where I have spent half my life pursuing the same elusive dream my father was never able to capture. The dream of the Iowa Baseball Confederacy. My father was not an easy man to live with. I always felt that my mother had some justification for her extended absences. Perhaps I have not been so easy to live with. Living with someone who is chasing a dream, like running after a butterfly across an endless meadow, a dream no one else sees or understands must be difficult.

Well, my father and I shared not only the dream, but he must have passed me something else through his genes: a fatal fascination for transient women.

11.

I remember a conversation I had with Gloria last week in Iowa City; I bumped into her on Dubuque Street and we walked over to Pearson's Drug Store for malts. Tall chocolate malts, thick as cement, served in perspiring glasses.

"Geez, Jack, you understand Stan better than anybody, maybe even me," Gloria said. "He looks up to you. If you could hear him talk about you all the time; he wishes he had your intellectual ability. He'd like to be able to read and understand things the way you do, you know. I bet Stan's never told you, but two summers ago, the year he turned thirty-four, I talked him into retiring."

"No, he didn't," I said.

"We'd wintered in South Carolina. He got a job in a warehouse; we had a nice apartment; I started thinking about getting pregnant. It was really nice, Stan home every night, me being able to cook supper for him, you know. And Stan was adjusting. He really was. He was nervous as a coyote in a pen but he was getting by. Then him and a couple of guys from work hooked up with a softball team. The league started in late April and at first I figured it wasn't such a bad idea. He could still play, you know, and I figured he wouldn't miss the game so much. The team was sponsored by Red Ryder's Pizza Parlor. The uniform-jerseys were cardinal-red, made of slippery material, with the silhouette of a square-jawed cowboy on the back where the numbers should have been.

"Oh God, Jack, it was sad to watch him. I mean he was the star of the team; he hit about .500 and they hardly ever lost. But it wasn't baseball and it didn't mean anything to him. The guys would all go back to Red Ryder's after a game and the owner would give them all the pizza they could eat and all the beer they could drink. After six weeks Stan was starting to develop a paunch on him.

"About the first of June he came home from work one evening and he was sitting on the edge of the bed putting his jersey on. I couldn't stand watching him no more; I reached over and I stopped him from pulling that slippery cloth down over his head. I grabbed hold of it, peeled it off him, tossed it into a corner, and leaned down and kissed him. I never seen Stan smile so hard, except when I said I'd marry him. I thought his face was gonna bust. 'Glory,' he says, 'I hear there's a Class B team down around Tidewater in a bad way for players. I think they might be glad to see a veteran outfielder . . .'

"And I says, 'I'm with you,' and next morning we were packed and heading south."

"He'll always get by, Gloria, as long as he's got you," and I reached down the counter and squeezed her hand.

"But I don't know what I'm gonna do, Jack. He was batting .220 and playing hurt, and his legs are gone. He was never fast but now he's like a big bear in the outfield. The fans boo him when he can't get to a long ball or a Texas leaguer."

"I'll do what I can," I told her. "But take care of him. He needs you."

"How are you and Sunny doing?" Gloria asked.

"Not very well, I'm afraid."

"She's been awful quiet; she looks down."

"She'll be gone again soon.

"I'm sorry, Jack."

"There's nothing anybody can do. She'll go and she'll come back. She'll be changed ever so subtly, like a piece of furniture that's been shipped across the country one more time. And I'll get a little more eccentric while she's gone. I'll haunt the University Library, do some more research on the Iowa Baseball Confederacy; the more my ideas are ridiculed the more stubborn I get, Gloria. Did I tell you I'm thinking of building an addition onto the front of the house — sort of a geodesic dome in the shape of a baseball?"

Gloria takes her lips away from the straw in her malt; she lifts her eyebrows; there is genuine concern in her eyes.

"When you have the name you might as well have the game. The university people, the baseball people, they all think I'm crazy to keep on pursuing the confederacy. The people in Onamata are worse; they don't know about the confederacy. They say, 'Jack Clarke's spent most of his life on some crazy research project. Something to do with baseball. Jack Clarke lives all alone in that big old house. Plays the piano at night and takes odd jobs when I hear he's got more money in the bank than he could spend in two lifetimes.' That's what they say, Gloria. That and, 'Jack Clarke had a wife and couldn't keep her.' "

12.

I got up early, left my empty house, spent all day in the University of Iowa library doing little research, sitting silent, dreaming of Sunny.

As I open the door to my house, smells of abandonment rush past me like bats. Though it is nearly July the air that meets my face is cold as a meat locker. Without Sunny, I don't think I will ever be able to live in these drafty rooms again. I close the door. The screen door makes a sharp snap. I need at least two doors between me and Sunny's memories and odours. In the fresh, moist warmth of the Iowa night I bed down on the cushions of the wide, white-painted porch swing.

Footfalls on the sidewalk and front steps awaken me. A dark silhouette stands before the front door, hand poised to knock.

"I'm over here, Stan," I whisper.

Stan starts as if someone has walked over his grave, throws his head back in a gesture of surprise.

"My god, you scared me, Jack. I was trying to decide how hard to knock."

I ease myself to a sitting position. The swing slices back and forth, cutting air. "Is it late?"

"Very," says Stan. "I can't sleep. Why are you out . . ."

"Sunny's gonc again," I say.

"I'm sorry, Jack. I know how much you care."

I nod. The porch and yard are silvered by moonlight.

"Makes my problem seem pretty small, I guess." Stan goes on. "A telegram arrived at the house last night. I told the club there was no phone there — I couldn't stand the thought of some secretary phoning to tell me I'd been cut."

"Is that what the telegr . . ."

"I haven't opened it. Gloria went to bed mad. I wouldn't let her open it either. Gloria's old lady looks at me with her lips all sewn shut . . . like I was something in a zoo."

"Do you want me to be there when you open it?"

"I don't know what I want. It was just laying there like a death sentence on that walnut-wood table in the front hall. Geez, but that's a depressing place, that hall. You seen that table, it's covered with a linen runner, with coloured tatting all around the edges. The baseboards are enamelled black and about a foot tall, and the newel post is black and shiny as a skull. I wanted to turn and run. I don't run from many things, Jackie, you know that. The telegram just lay there on the linen runner like a yellow stain, evil, liquid, changing shape. Gloria's old lady was standing there, her hands clasped in front of her, her hair pulled back until her eyes bugged out.

" 'For goodness sakes open it,' Gloria said. But I wouldn't touch it or let her touch it. I mean I *know* what's in it, Jackie. I'm not dumb. There was something rotten in the air when they put me on the disabled list. The manager had a crafty look about him. I'm thirty-six years old, and I been playing hurt. I've been released. I know it.''

''Maybe it's not . . .''

''I *know*,'' Stan says emphatically. ''You understand better than anybody, Jack. I need to go for a walk, or a drive. I want you to come with me.''

''Okay,'' I say.

''Man, you should have come to our place when you found Sunny was gone. You shouldn't be alone.''

''Let's go,'' I say, standing up. The arc of the swing lessens until it is barely trembling.

''It's not fair,'' Stan says, as we make our way down the silent, leafy streets, the air slightly sweet from the last lilacs of the season.

''What isn't?'' I reply.

''I want to go into Iowa City,'' Stan says. ''My car's just around the corner. I parked there a while ago and tried to walk it off, the way I do when I take a foul-tip on the shin. But it didn't work.''

We try to close the doors quietly. We are probably the only people awake in the whole town of Onamata.

''This cast is supposed to stay on for ten more days,'' he says, banging the white plaster against the steering wheel as he turns the car out onto the silent, bluey highway. ''But I bet I could get it off in seven if I concentrated. You heal faster if you concentrate all your energy on the sore part of your body, did you know that?''

''No.''

''Well, you can. A week and I'll be good as new. It was unfair as hell for them to let me go instead of letting me work my way back from the disabled list. I've still got a few good years left in me. I might still make it to the majors. I know I'll never be a starter, but I could still be a utility man, fill in a game here and a game there, pinch hit once in a while, play defence in the late innings. I've still got a few years left in me, haven't I, Jackie? Thirty-six ain't too old, is it?''

''It's not too old,'' I say. I look in the rear-view mirror

expecting to see Gloria's form in the back seat, the glow of Sunny's cigarette.

"You know, yesterday, when I went into Iowa City, I went to see Gloria's brother, Dmetro, went down to the railroad yard and he showed me around. I only did it to please Gloria and her old lady. Dmetro's a checker there in the yards. I'm not sure what he really does — they don't let him touch the switches or nothing like that — he has a chart and a clipboard and I think he makes sure the right cars are on the right trains. He started that job the day after he turned fifteen. His old man made him quit school and got him that job. Made Gloria quit on her fifteenth birthday too, but she went back after she got out on her own. Her old man worked for forty-nine years for the flour mill; he died six months after they retired him. Dmetro's my age; he's got a job for life. He'll never get laid off or bumped or anything. I guess he's happy. 'I can do my job in my sleep,' he says. 'I don't have to think or nothing.'"

I want to say something to comfort Stan, but the right words are elusive. Instead, I gesture helplessly with my hands.

"Dmetro offered to get me a job there. Did I tell you that? Gloria wants me to take it. I mean the three of them set it up. They think I'm so dumb I don't know. I'd be a kind of gofer to start with, working the midnight shift, not very steady at all." Stan pauses, looks over at me.

"You know, Jack," he goes on, "last week I drove up to the stadium in Iowa City, I was running in the outfield, doing stretching exercises on the grass, stuff like that, when I happened to look up at the sky. There were little white puffs of cloud all across it, like a cat stepped in milk and then walked across the blue. I thought it was so beautiful I told Dmetro about it. He just stared at me. 'I ain't looked at the sky in ten years,' he said. I believed him." Stan guides the car with the tips of the fingers that peek from the white cast and slaps his other meaty hand on the dashboard.

"There was something else too, something that really bothered me, Jackie. Dmetro was telling me the names of the spur lines, the dead-end tracks where they store boxcars or move them in and out of the yards. There was the Exxon Spur, the Texaco Spur, and the Miller Spur that runs right down to the brewery. There was the Ice House Spur from when they used to cut ice from the Iowa River and store it in sawdust. Then there was a spur out at the edge of the yard that had ties piled across it. Dmetro told me they use that one to store broken boxcars. He didn't name it at all, but later he spotted a boxcar with a cracked wheel and said it would have to be moved to the Baseball Spur."

"Where's that?" I asked, pricking up my ears.

"Back in the old days, according to Dmetro, the Baseball Spur used to run out of town for a mile or more to a ballpark. On Saturday and Sunday afternoons whole families used to get dressed up and pack picnic lunches and catch the train out to the baseball game. His old man said there used to be two trips both ways. He remembered it, though he never went himself. But they tore down the grandstand back in the twenties, and the railroad figured it was cheaper to let the roadbed rot than to tear up the tracks. Some junk dealer eventually made off with most of the steel, but the track still runs a few hundred yards, and you could still follow the roadbed if you really tried. All that's used of the Baseball Spur now is the hundred yards or so inside the railroad yard."

Stan eases the car to a stop on a dark side street not far from the railroad yard. Again, we are both careful as we close the doors.

"Hey, Jackie," Stan says in a voice too loud for the night. "Remember how in high school I spotted that the West Branch pitcher stood a certain way on the rubber when he was gonna throw a curve?"

"I remember," I say.

"And I wouldn't tell anybody else what I knew — just you and me?"

"I remember."

" 'If I stand with a bat on my right shoulder, it's gonna be a curve,' I told you. You whacked a triple to deep centre."

"The only triple I ever hit," I say.

"Yeah, you were never much with the bat, were you? Well, he got two quick strikes on me before I saw him set his foot in a certain position. I took a deep breath and waited. The ball was still rising when it cleared the fence, and those two runs put the game right out of reach.''

The railroad yards loom in front of us as we top a rise: acres of boxcars, and bluey ribbons of track criss-crossing like tangles of wool.

''Is this where we're going?'' I ask.

''Yeah, I want you to see this place, Jackie.''

In the yard, outdoor lights sway slightly, casting long, eerie shadows. The roundhouse hulks in front of us, high as a grain elevator. There are men in coveralls scurrying about, the air is steely-smelling, full of grease and hot metal. Bright blue stars from welding torches bloom in the yellowish light. The door of the roundhouse gapes wide. Inside there are figures in white tee-shirts climbing like ants over a tall black engine. No one pays any attention to us.

''We fit right in,'' Stan says.

He's right. We are both wearing white cotton tee-shirts and jeans. A row of picks and sledge-hammers lean haphazardly against the corrugated metal wall of a shed. Stan stoops, picks up a sledge-hammer, hoists it on his shoulder like a bat. I bend and pick one up. It is heavier than I imagined.

''The Baseball Spur is way back here,'' Stan says, pointing between two dark rows of boxcars.

There are two cars on the spur, each with a wheel partially broken away, the fractured surface of each bright as a new coin. We amble past the damaged boxcars, walk between the rails where ankle-high grass heavy with dew wets our shoes and cuffs.

''This feels good,'' Stan says, hefting the sledge and moving into a batting crouch. 'Rogalski in the on-deck circle,' he announces. 'Rogalski beat out Dave Winfield for the centrefield spot on the Yankees. It's a shame to have a player of Winfield's calibre sitting on the bench,' the Yankee manager said, 'but Rogalski's just too good.' ''

We come to the edge of the railroad yards and the end of the Baseball Spur. There is a barricade across the tracks, consisting of a sturdy six-by-eight driven spike-like into the roadbed on each side of the track, then five ties stacked across the tracks and bolted at each end to the six-by-eights. I walk behind the barricade where the spur passes into a tangle of raspberry canes, willows, and saplings. In the distance I see a tiny scratch of silver where wind and snow have scrubbed the rust away. A moonbeam touches down on it like a wand and it shimmers bright as a needle in the creamy warmth of the Iowa night.

"See, what did I tell you. It's here just like I said it was. Think about all the history here, Jackie. Doesn't it just make you tingle. Like the first time I knew a girl was gonna let me put my hand down her blouse," and Stan grins wildly, his face turned up toward the moonlight.

"Hey, Jackie, do you remember how when we were kids there used to be ads on the backs of comic books and sports magazines. I don't remember who sponsored them, but they were for groups — you know, churches and boy scouts and things like that. They wanted to see who could sell the most salve, or Christmas cards, or wrapping paper. And the grand prize for the group that sold the most was a baseball field. They claimed they'd come out to your town and build you a baseball field, you know, level it, sod it, put up a backstop, I don't know if they built an outfield fence or not. But they always showed a picture on the back of the magazine with new bases sitting out there white as Leghorn hens and the grass an unreal green, a heavenly green, and the whole field covered in kids wearing red-and-white uniforms. You know what I always dreamed, Jackie? That I was a charity, or a church group, and I sold the most stuff, and they came and built me a baseball field."

I'd like to step around the barricade and hug Stan, if men did that sort of thing, and tell him I understand his fears, and how trapped he feels, and that I appreciate his dreams, and have had a few of my own. But it's better not to be aware of too many of the workings of the world. My curse is that I understood too much, at least about Sunny. It's better to be like Stan, to be continually amazed. Stan is always amazed by what happens to him, but not surprised. I'm still surprised by life, and I know that isn't good.

The barricade across the Baseball Spur has been put there to stop any boxcar that might manage to coast that far. Stan and I grin at each other as if we've just completed a double steal. The moon is so bright that the yards look almost beautiful in the distance. The tracks are blue and silver and gold, while only feet away they are coated in rust and disappear into weeds and wild grass. There is just a hint of ground mist in the ditches and there are mosquitoes purring about my face.

Stan squares his shoulders, takes the sledge and swings it back sideways as if he were ringing a gong, and brings it forward landing a mighty blow to one of the ties. The barricade barely budges. But Stan swings again and again, chipping the ties, splintering them, breaking them away from the blue-headed bolts. He sets down the hammer and lifts the broken ties one by one and tosses them into the ditch. Each time a little puff of coolness, sweet with the odours of grass, rises and envelops us.

How I Got My Nickname

How I Got My Nickname

For Brian Fawcett,
whose story "My Career with the Leafs"
inspired this story.

In the summer of 1951, the summer before I was to start Grade 12, my polled Hereford calf, Simon Bolivar, won Reserve Grand Champion at the Des Moines, All-Iowa Cattle Show and Summer Exposition. My family lived on a hobby-farm near Iowa City. My father who taught classics at Coe College in Cedar Rapids, and in spite of that was still the world's number one baseball fan, said I deserved a reward — I also had a straight A average in Grade 11 and had published my first short story that spring. My father phoned his friend Robert Fitzgerald (Fitzgerald, an eminent translator, sometimes phoned my father late at night and they talked about various ways of interpreting the tougher parts of *The Iliad*) and two weeks later I found myself in Fitzgerald's spacious country home outside of New York City, sharing the lovely old house with the Fitzgeralds, their endless supply of children, and a young writer from Georgia named Flannery

O'Connor. Miss O'Connor was charming, and humorous in an understated way, and I wish I had talked with her more. About the third day I was there I admitted to being a published writer and Miss O'Connor said "You must show me some of your stories." I never did. I was seventeen, overweight, diabetic, and bad-complexioned. I alternated between being terminally shy and obnoxiously brazen. I was nearly always shy around the Fitzgeralds and Miss O'Connor. I was also terribly homesick, which made me appear more silent and outlandish than I knew I was. I suspect I am the model for Enoch Emery, the odd, lonely country boy in Miss O'Connor's novel *Wise Blood*. But that is another story.

On a muggy August morning, the first day of a Giant home stand at the Polo Grounds, I prepared to travel into New York. I politely invited Miss O'Connor to accompany me, but she, even at that early date had to avoid sunlight and often wore her wide-brimmed straw hat, even indoors. I set off much too early and though terrified of the grimy city and shadows that seemed to lurk in every doorway, arrived at the Polo Grounds over two hours before game time. It was raining gently and I was one of about two dozen fans in the ballpark. A few players were lethargically playing catch, a coach was hitting fungos to three players in right field. I kept edging my way down the rows of seats until I was right behind the Giants dugout.

The Giants were thirteen games behind the Dodgers and the pennant race appeared all but over. A weasel-faced bat boy, probably some executive's nephew, I thought, noticed me staring wide-eyed at the players and the playing field. He curled his lip at me, then stuck out his tongue. He mouthed the words "Take a picture, it'll last longer," adding something at the end that I could only assume to be uncomplimentary.

Fired by the insult I suddenly mustered all my bravado and called out "Hey, Mr Durocher?" Leo Durocher, the Giants manager, had been standing in the third base coach's box not looking at anything in particular. I was really impressed. That's the grand thing about baseball, I thought. Even a manager in a pennant race can take time to daydream. He didn't hear me. But the bat boy did, and stuck out his tongue again.

I was overpowered by my surroundings. Though I'd seen a lot of major league baseball I'd never been in the Polo Grounds before. The history of the place . . . "Hey, Mr Durocher," I shouted.

Leo looked up at me with a baleful eye. He needed a shave, and the lines around the corners of his mouth looked like ruts.

"What is it, Kid?"

"Could I hit a few?" I asked hopefully, as if I was begging to stay up an extra half hour. "You know, take a little batting practice?"

"Sure, Kid. Why not?" and Leo smiled with one corner of his mouth. "We want all our fans to feel like part of the team."

From the box seat where I'd been standing, I climbed up on the roof of the dugout and Leo helped me down onto the field.

Leo looked down into the dugout. The rain was stopping. On the other side of the park a few of the Phillies were wandering onto the field. "Hey, George," said Leo, staring into the dugout, "throw the kid here a few pitches. Where are you from, son?"

It took me a few minutes to answer because I experienced this strange, lightheaded feeling, as if I had too much sun. "Near to Iowa City, Iowa," I managed to say in a small voice. Then "You're going to win the pennant, Mr. Durocher. I just know you are."

"Well, thanks, Kid," said Leo modestly, "we'll give it our best shot."

George was George Bamberger, a stocky rookie who had seen limited action. "Bring the kid a bat, Andy," Leo said to the bat boy. The bat boy curled his lip at me but slumped into the dugout, as Bamberger and Sal Yvars tossed the ball back and forth.

The bat boy brought me a black bat. I was totally unprepared for how heavy it was. I lugged it to the plate and stepped into the right hand batter's box. Bamberger delivered an easy, looping, batting-practice pitch. I drilled it back up the middle.

"Pretty good, Kid," I heard Durocher say.

Bamberger threw another easy one and I fouled it off. The third pitch was a little harder. I hammered it to left.

"Curve him," said Durocher.

He curved me. Even through my thick glasses the ball looked as big as a grapefruit, illuminated like a small moon. I whacked it and it hit the right field wall on one bounce.

"You weren't supposed to hit that one," said Sal Yvars.

"You're pretty good, Kid," shouted Durocher from the third base box. "Give him your best stuff, George."

Over the next fifteen minutes I batted about .400 against George Bamberger, and Roger Bowman, including a home run into the left centrefield stands. The players on the Giants bench were watching me with mild interest often looking up from the books most of them were reading.

"I'm gonna put the infield out now," said Durocher. "I want you to run out some of your hits."

Boy, here I was batting against the real New York Giants. I wished I'd worn a new shirt instead of the horizontally striped red and white one I had on, which made me look heftier than I really was. Bowman threw a sidearm curve and I almost broke my back swinging at it. But he made the mistake of coming right back with the same pitch. I looped it behind third where it landed soft as a sponge, and trickled off toward the stands — I'd seen the play hundreds of times — a stand-up double. But when I was still twenty feet from second base Eddie Stanky was waiting with the ball. "Slide!" somebody yelled, but I just skidded to a stop, stepping out of the baseline to avoid the tag. Stanky whapped me anyway, a glove to the ribs that would have made Rocky Marciano or Ezzard Charles proud.

When I got my wind back Durocher was standing, hands on hips, staring down at me.

"Why the hell didn't you slide, Kid?"

"I can't," I said, a little indignantly. "I'm diabetic, I have to avoid stuff like that. If I cut myself, or even bruise badly, it takes forever to heal."

"Oh," said Durocher. "Well, I guess that's okay then."

"You shouldn't tag people so hard," I said to Stanky. "Somebody could get hurt."

"Sorry, Kid," said Stanky. I don't think he apologized very

often. I noticed that his spikes were filed. But I found later that he knew a lot about F. Scott Fitzgerald. His favourite story was "Babylon Revisited" so that gave us a lot in common; I was a real Fitzgerald fan; Stanky and I became friends even though both he and Durocher argued against reading *The Great Gatsby* as an allegory.

"Where'd you learn your baseball?" an overweight coach who smelled strongly of snuff, and bourbon, said to me.

"I live near Iowa City, Iowa," I said in reply.

Everyone wore question marks on their faces. I saw I'd have to elaborate. "Iowa City is within driving distance of Chicago, St. Louis, Milwaukee, and there's minor league ball in Cedar Rapids, Omaha, Kansas City. Why there's barely a weekend my dad and I don't go somewhere to watch professional baseball."

"Watch?" said Durocher.

"Well, we talk about it some too. My father is a real student of the game. Of course we only talk in Latin when we're on the road, it's a family custom."

"Latin?" said Durocher.

"Say something in Latin," said Whitey Lockman, who had wandered over from first base.

"The Etruscans have invaded all of Gaul," I said in Latin.

"Their fortress is on the banks of the river," said Bill Rigney, who had been filling in at third base.

"Velle est posse," I said.

"Where there's a will there's a way," translated Durocher.

"Drink Agri Cola . . ." I began.

"The farmer's drink," said Sal Yvars, slapping me on the back, but gently enough not to bruise me. I guess I looked a little surprised.

"Most of us are more than ballplayers," said Alvin Dark, who had joined us. "In fact the average player on this squad is fluent in three languages."

"*Watch?*" said Durocher, getting us back to baseball. "You *watch* a lot of baseball, but where do you play?"

"I've never played in my life," I replied. "But I have a

photographic memory. I just watch how different players hold their bat, how they stand. I try to emulate Enos Slaughter and Joe Di Maggio.''

"Can you field?'' said Durocher.

"No.''

"No?''

"I've always just watched the hitters. I've never paid much attention to the fielders.''

He stared at me as if I had spoken to him in an unfamiliar foreign language.

"Everybody fields,'' he said. "What position do you play?''

"I've never played,'' I reiterated. "My health is not very good.''

"Cripes,'' he said, addressing the sky. "You drop a second Ted Williams on me and he tells me he can't field.'' Then to Alvin Dark: "Hey, Darky, throw a few with the kid here. Get him warmed up.''

In the dugout Durocher pulled a thin, black glove from an equipment bag and tossed it to me. I dropped it. The glove had no discernable padding in it. The balls Dark threw hit directly on my hand, when I caught them, which was about one out of three. "Ouch!'' I cried. "Don't throw so hard.''

"Sorry, Kid,'' said Alvin Dark and threw the next one a little easier. If I really heaved I could just get the ball back to him. I have always thrown like a non-athletic girl. I could feel my hand bloating inside the thin glove. After about ten pitches, I pulled my hand out. It looked as though it had been scalded.

"Don't go away, Kid,'' said Leo. "In fact why don't you sit in the dugout with me. What's your name anyway?''

"W.P. Kinsella,'' I said.

"Your friends call you W?''

"My father calls me William, and my mother . . .'' but I let my voice trail off. I didn't think Leo Durocher would want to know my mother still called me Bunny.

"Jeez,'' said Durocher. "You need a nickname, Kid. Bad.''

"I'll work on it,'' I said.

I sat right beside Leo Durocher all that stifling afternoon in the Polo Grounds as the Giants swept a doubleheader from the

Phils, the start of a sixteen-game streak that was to lead to the October 3, 1951 Miracle of Coogan's Bluff. I noticed right away that the Giants were all avid readers. In fact, the *New York Times* Best Seller Lists, and the *Time* and *Newsweek* lists of readable books and an occasional review were taped to the walls of the dugout. When the Giants were in the field I peeked at the covers of the books the players sometimes read between innings. Willie Mays was reading *The Cruel Sea* by Nicholas Monsarrat. Between innings Sal Maglie was deeply involved in Carson McCullers's new novel *The Ballad of the Sad Cafe*. "I sure wish we could get that Cousin Lyman to be our mascot," he said to me when he saw me eyeing the bookjacket, referring to the hunchbacked dwarf who was the main character in the novel. "We need something to inspire us," he added. Alvin Dark slammed down his copy of *Requiem for a Nun* and headed for the on-deck circle.

When the second game ended, a sweaty and sagging Leo Durocher took me by the arm. "There's somebody I want you to meet, Kid," he said. Horace Stoneham's office was furnished in wine-coloured leather sofas and overstuffed horsehair chairs. Stoneham sat behind an oak desk as big as the dugout, enveloped in cigar smoke.

"I've got a young fellow here I think we should sign for the stretch drive," Durocher said. "He can't field or run, but he's as pure a hitter as I've ever seen. He'll make a hell of a pinch hitter."

"I suppose you'll want a bonus?" growled Stoneham.

"I do have something in mind," I said. Even Durocher was not nearly so jovial as he had been. Both men stared coldly at me. Durocher leaned over and whispered something to Stoneham.

"How about $6,000," Stoneham said.

"What I'd really like . . ." I began.

"Alright, $10,000, but not a penny more."

"Actually, I'd like to meet Bernard Malamud. I thought you could maybe invite him down to the park. Maybe get him to sign a book for me?" They both looked tremendously relieved.

"Bernie and me and this kid Salinger are having supper this

evening," said Durocher. "Why don't you join us?"

"You mean J.D. Salinger?" I said.

"Jerry's a big Giant fan," he said. "The team Literary Society read *Catcher in the Rye* last month. We had a panel discussion on it for eight hours on the train to St. Louis."

Before I signed the contract I phoned my father.

"No reason you can't postpone your studies until the end of the season," he said. "It'll be good experience for you. You'll gather a lot of material you can write about later. Besides, baseball players are the real readers of America."

I got my first hit off Warren Spahn, a solid single up the middle. Durocher immediately replaced me with a pinch runner. I touched Ralph Branca for a double, the ball went over Duke Snider's head, hit the wall and bounced half way back to the infield. Anyone else would have had an inside the park homer. I wheezed into second and was replaced. I got into 38 of the final 42 games. I hit 11 for 33, and was walked four times. And hit once. That was the second time I faced Warren Spahn. He threw a swishing curve that would have gone behind me if I hadn't backed into it. I slouched off toward first holding my ribs.

"You shouldn't throw at batters like that," I shouted, "someone could get seriously hurt. I'm diabetic, you know." I'd heard that Spahn was into medical texts and interested in both human and veterinary medicine.

"Sorry," he shouted back. "If I'd known I wouldn't have thrown at you. I've got some good linament in the clubhouse. Come see me after the game. By the way I hear you're trying to say that *The Great Gatsby* is an allegory."

"The way I see it, it is," I said. "You see the eyes of the optometrist on the billboard are really the eyes of God looking down on a fallen world . . ."

"Alright, alright," said the umpire, Beans Reardon, "let's get on with the game. By the way, Kid, I don't think it's an allegory either. A statement on the human condition, perhaps. But not an allegory."

The players wanted to give me some nickname other than "Kid." Someone suggested "Ducky" in honour of my running style. "Fats" said somebody else. I made a note to remove his bookmark between innings. Several other suggestions were downright obscene. Baseball players, in spite of their obsession with literature and the arts, often have a bawdy sense of humour.

"How about 'Moonlight,' " I suggested. I'd read about an old time player who stopped for a cup of coffee with the Giants half a century before, who had that nickname.

"What the hell for?" said Monty Irvin, who in spite of the nickname preferred to be called Monford or even by his second name Merrill. "You got to have a reason for a nickname. You got to earn it. Still, anything's better than W.P."

"It was only a suggestion," I said. I made a mental note not to tell Monford what I knew about *his* favourite author, Erskine Caldwell.

As it turned out I didn't earn a nickname until the day we won the pennant.

As every baseball fan knows the Giants went into the bottom of the ninth in the deciding game of the pennant playoff trailing the Dodgers 4-1.

"Don't worry," I said to Durocher, "everything's going to work out." If he heard me he didn't let on.

But was everything going to work out? And what part was I going to play in it? Even though I'd contributed to the Giants' amazing stretch drive, I didn't belong. Why am I here? I kept asking myself. I had some vague premonition that I was about to change history. I mean I wasn't a ballplayer. I was a writer. Here I was about to go into Grade 12 and I was already planning to do my master's thesis on F. Scott Fitzgerald.

I didn't have time to worry further as Alvin Dark singled. Don Mueller, in his excitement had carried his copy of *The Mill on the Floss* out to the on-deck circle. He set the resin bag on top of it, stalked to the plate and singled, moving Dark to second.

I was flabbergasted when Durocher called Monford Irvin back and said to me "Get in there, Kid."

It was at that moment that I knew why I was there. I would indeed change history. One stroke of the bat and the score would be tied. I eyed the left field stands as I nervously swung two bats to warm up. I was nervous but not scared. I never doubted my prowess for one moment. Years later Johnny Bench summed it up for both athletes and writers when he talked about a successful person having to have an *inner conceit*. It never occurred to me until days later that I might have hit into a double or triple play, thus ending it and *really* changing history.

When I did take my place in the batter's box, I pounded the plate and glared out at Don Newcombe. I wished that I shaved so I could give him a stubble-faced stare of contempt. He curved me and I let it go by for a ball. I fouled the next pitch high into the first base stands. A fastball was low. I fouled the next one outside third. I knew he didn't want to go to a full count: I crowded the plate a little looking for the fastball. He curved me. Nervy. But the curveball hung, sat out over the plate like a cantaloupe. I waited an extra millisecond before lambasting it. In that instant the ball broke in on my hands; it hit the bat right next to my right hand. It has been over thirty years but I still wake deep in the night, my hands vibrating, burning from Newcombe's pitch. The bat shattered into kindling. The ball flew in a polite loop as if it had been tossed by a five-year-old; it landed soft as a creampuff in Peewee Reese's glove. One out.

I slumped back to the bench.

"Tough luck, Kid," said Durocher, patting my shoulder. "There'll be other chances to be a hero."

"Thanks, Leo," I said.

Whitey Lockman doubled. Dark scored. Mueller hurt himself sliding into third. Rafael Noble went in to run for Mueller. Charlie Dressen replaced Newcombe with Ralph Branca. Bobby Thomson swung bats in the on-deck circle.

As soon as umpire Jorda called time-in, Durocher leapt to his feet, and before Bobby Thomson could take one step toward the plate, Durocher called him back.

"Don't do that!" I yelled, suddenly knowing why I was *really* there. But Durocher ignored me. He was beckoning with a big-knuckled finger to another reserve player, a big outfielder who was tearing up the American Association when they brought him up late in the year. He was 5 for 8 as a pinch hitter.

Durocher was already up the dugout steps heading toward the umpire to announce the change. The outfielder from the American Association was making his way down the dugout, hopping along over feet and ankles. He'd be at the top of the step by the time Durocher reached the umpire.

As he skipped by me, the last person between Bobby Thomson and immortality, I stuck out my foot. The outfielder from the American Association went down like he'd been poleaxed. He hit his face on the top step of the dugout, crying out loud enough to attract Durocher's attention.

The trainer hustled the damaged player to the clubhouse. Durocher waved Bobby Thomson to the batter's box. And the rest is history. After the victory celebration I announced my retirement blaming it on a damaged wrist. I went back to Iowa and listened to the World Series on the radio.

All I have to show that I ever played in the major leagues is my one-line entry in *The Baseball Encyclopedia:*

W.P. KINSELLA   Kinsella, William Patrick "Tripper" BR TR 5'9" 185 lbs. B. Apr. 14, 1934 Onamata, Ia.

	G	AB	H	2B	3B	HR	HR %	R	RBI	BB	SO	EA	BA	Pinch Hit AB	H
1951 NY N	38	33	11	2	0	2	6.0	0	8	4	4	0	.333	33	11

I got my outright release in the mail the week after the World Series ended. Durocher had scrawled across the bottom: "Good luck, Kid. By the way, *The Great Gatsby* is *not* an allegory."

Bud and Tom

Bud and Tom

There are two reasons why I have no fear of death. The first is that I suffered a critical illness when I was ten years old. I had strep throat and for more than a week hovered between life and death. Although my throat hurt terribly even that pain dissipated as I drifted closer to death. I felt as if I was swathed in pink cotton batting; I was warm and calm and happy. At least once I was outside my body, viewing the room from the ceiling, noticing how my body was so flat it made barely a bulge in the bed spread, how my feet extended no more than half the length of the hospital bed. I saw my mother seated beside the bed wearing a housedress and a small blue hat. I was never afraid of dying. I was not displeased when the far away voices told me I was to be treated with penicillin, a wonder drug, just recently put into common use, but I was not thrilled either. All my life I have enjoyed cuddling down into a soft warm bed. I know that is what death will be like and I am not afraid.

The second reason is that at fourteen I faced death head-on and came away unafraid. My parents, who I don't think had ever left me alone, went on an overnight trip to a place where my father had the contract to plaster and stucco a new hotel.

My Uncle Bud and I cooked supper, ate, washed the dishes, then sat down to play cards at the kitchen table. We were in the middle of a game of cribbage, when, at about eight o'clock my uncle leaned back on the scarlet coloured plastic kitchen chair, tipped his head far back at an unnatural angle, sighed once, and was dead. There was nothing frightening about the experience. There was no question that he was dead. I remember thinking that I had had scarier experiences walking home from the bus through the pitch black streets of Great Falls. I went into the hall where the telephone was located, found the number for Smith's Ambulance on the list of Emergency Numbers written in my mother's neat hand on the inside cover of the telephone book, called them, gave them the address, explained that I was quite certain my uncle was dead.

"How old are you?" said the man at Smith's Ambulance.

"Fourteen," I replied.

"How can you be sure he's dead?"

"He has no pulse, and I *can* tell."

"The ambulance will be right there."

And it was within ten minutes. The attendants didn't even move him from the chair. They felt his wrist and neck and said "What you need is an undertaker."

"I told the guy on the phone," I said.

"You know one to call," said the attendant.

"We deal with Foster and McGarvey," I said, as if death was a regular occurrence in our family.

Within an hour a hearse arrived at our front door and two black-suited men placed Uncle Bud on a stretcher and carried him down the steep front steps to the hearse.

I listened to the radio for a while. Frankie Laine was singing, "My heart goes where the wild goose goes . . ." Then I went to bed.

I stayed home from school the next morning, not because I wanted to but because I thought it might be disrespectful to just leave a note on the door for my parents.

"Oh, how terrible for you," my father said when I greeted him with the information. He put his arm around me and continued to gush for several minutes.

"Did you eat a good breakfast?" my mother wanted to know.

They were both surprised that I had dispatched the body to the correct funeral home, and that I hadn't called in neighbours, or relatives, or at least had a friend over to spend the night with me.

"It was no big deal," I said. "He just died."

Uncle Bud was my father's oldest brother. He had lived with us for about six months. We knew he had a heart condition but no one thought he was going to die so soon. He was only sixty.

We were late for the funeral. Car trouble. My father's 1939 Terraplane, wide-fendered, the smooth grey of weathered rock, started coughing and lurching before we were more than a few blocks from home. My father guided the car to the Ford dealership in downtown Great Falls, and soon a mechanic wearing a filthy trough-cap advertising something called Veedol, and wearing grey-striped railroad coveralls, had his head buried in the engine. My mother sat primly in the car; she was wearing a new, blueberry-coloured hat with a blueberry-coloured veil. My father was wearing his good suit, a dirt-coloured pin-stripe, a tweed cap, and gray spats.

My father and I paced in circles on the crumbling cement floor, stopping occasionally to peer over the mechanic's shoulder. My father kept extracting his pocket watch on its brown shoelace lead, checking the time. The funeral was at a small town forty miles outside Great Falls. By the time we wriggled our way out of the city, it would be an hour's drive, perhaps more in the cold, October drizzle.

"We'll make it in time," my father assured me more than once, as if I needed assurance. I tried to look as though I was anxious for the car to be fixed and for us to be on our way. In fact I was hoping the gas line would stay plugged forever. It wasn't that I didn't want to attend Uncle Bud's funeral; it was that I was supposed to be a pallbearer. In that way families have of never discussing serious matters with children, it was rather mysteriously decided, I suppose by my father and his sisters, that Bud's nephews would be the pallbearers. Pallbearer is a frightening word. How would I know what to do?

when to lift the coffin? how to stand? where to stand? Though I am now well into middle age, I have never been a pallbearer, never intend to be. It turned out there were only four nephews within driving distance of the funeral. A cousin was pressed into service, and a school-mate of his, one who had known my uncle, became the sixth.

"You be sure to get in the middle," my father said to me, "the ones on the four corners take the most weight. After all you're the youngest."

Uncle Bud's real name was Patrick. It was my father who gave him his nickname. My father was the baby of the family, his attempts to refer to Patrick as his brother resulted in Patrick being known as Bud for the rest of his life.

The car was eventually fixed and we headed out into the vile weather. Rain pelted down, propelled by a raw wind; the windows of the ten-year-old Terraplane fogged up; the car fish-tailed eerily as we travelled first on pavement, then gravel, and finally on dirt roads, greasy as cookie sheets. The ditches brimmed with cold, iron-coloured water, the fenceposts were black and sodden. In the fields, stubble glistened sullenly, remarkably yellow against the puddled earth.

I remember thinking during the drive that it mattered little whether we got there or not. Catholics did not open the coffin at their services. What reason could there be for going to the funeral if you couldn't get a last look at the deceased? I had been to a number of funerals, including my grandfather on my mother's side, where I filed past the coffin, glimpsing my grandfather's bluish face and blue-grey hair.

"A tough old bird," my father said of him, "eighty-six years old and it took getting run over by a car to kill him."

Looking back, I am appalled at how little I know about the history of my family. I knew only that one grandparent, and if either my father or mother knew their grandparents, or even knew of them, they never mentioned them. My mother's family came to Montana from Norwich, Connecticut, in the early 1900s. A Rose Eliot married a Thomas Elliott, and settled on a homestead near Havre, Montana, then moved to a town called

Floweree, a few miles north of Great Falls, where my mother and her sister were raised.

My father's family came from the Black Hills of North Dakota, arriving in Montana about 1900 and settling north and west of Great Falls. My father said that my grandparents, Patrick Kinsella Sr. and Ellen Murphy, met on a boat while emigrating from Ireland. I don't know what part of Ireland they came from. If my father knew he never mentioned it. He was a staunch supporter of Irish Independence. I don't think the IRA had been organized yet, perhaps Sinn Fein was what he supported. When he was happy he sang Irish revolutionary songs like "The Wearin' 'O The Green," and I remember once, when I was very ill, as a small child, he sang a song about the Irish patriot John Martin Duffy, the words of which I cannot recall. When I was a little older but we were still living on a farm, I remember in the dimness of the coffee-smelling General Store, my father turning his back to me as he surreptitiously stuffed a few dollars into a purplish envelope. I then remember him buying a number of what he called "overseas" stamps for the letter.

I realize as I write that I have raised my daughters as I was raised. I have not even told them the stories I am shaping here. They do not know of my uncle dying at the kitchen table. My father was dead before they were born. History shrinks.

We arrived just as the procession was leaving the church and winding its way toward the graveyard. We pulled up across the street, the car very nearly sliding into a brimming ditch. The coffin was now being navigated around the corner of the church, heading for the graveyard at the rear, hoisted on the shoulders of five young men. I sighed with relief.

"Catch up with them," said my father. I had no desire to do so. Despite his nudging my arm, encouraging me to hurry, I took my mother's arm as we crossed the slippery street and made our way alongside the church. Not until we reached the cemetery, until I had seen the five pallbearers lay down their burden at graveside, did I take my place, being sure to break into the middle on the side with only two pallbearers. The rain streaked my glasses and made dark stains on the wine-coloured jacket I wore.

I remember nothing that was said at the gravesite. I do remember being cold and hoping my jacket wouldn't be permanently stained. A very old, white-maned priest mumbled away in what was probably Latin. Uncle Bud and all of my father's relatives were Catholic. My father was the black sheep of the family. Early in life he renounced the Church, married a Protestant, revelled in repeating the most vile priest and nun stories imaginable, and denounced the Pope and the Catholic church in general at every opportunity. I suspect it was only because I had been alone with Uncle Bud when he died that I was allowed to be a pallbearer. There must have been a good deal of whispering and consternation about allowing a heathen to participate, even in a minor way in one of their rituals. On the other hand, I suspect the more optimistic relatives suggested that the exposure would do me good, perhaps draw me into the fold.

After the graveside service, we left the sodden cemetery and walked to my Uncle Tom's house, which was only three doors south of the church. Uncle Tom was married to my father's oldest sister. They had recently sold their farm and retired to this hamlet of ten houses, a false-fronted general store and tall white church.

The house was squat and frame, heated only by a big, black kitchen stove. Every inch of the living room was stuffed with furniture. The box-like chairs and overstuffed sofa were covered with bright-patterned shawls, both knitted and crocheted. There were decorative pillows everywhere, some velvet with bright punchwork flowers, others of silk or satin with sentimental mottos, religious quotes, or the bland, long-suffering face of Jesus outlined in sparkling paint. The cold interior of the house was jammed with people from the community and from nearby towns. The kitchen table was covered with chocolate cakes, and plates of sliced roast beef and cold fried chicken; there were salmon, ham, and egg salad sandwiches. Aunt Lizzie perked coffee on the giant black range, using her own blue-enamelled coffee pot, and a more modern two-piece aluminum-coloured one, brought by one of her daughters.

Unfortunately, I was somewhat of a curiosity. Most of the neighbours, even a few of the relatives had never seen me, or not seen me since I was a baby. I was patted and mauled, kissed and fawned over. Those who knew about me being with Uncle Bud when he died, offered condolences in awkward, inarticulate snatches. The women were mostly middle-aged, big bosomed, and had on too much cheap perfume, lily-of-the-valley being the favourite. Most wore dresses with huge red-and-white, or red-and-blue flowers, or they wore red-and-green crêpes, and veiled hats, ranging from quite simplistic to monstrosities the size of trailer tires.

When Uncle Tom saw me he put his heavy arm around my shoulder for a moment.

"You're a very brave boy," he said. "You did what you had to do." Then he squinted his left eye and added, "You'd think he could have at least picked nice weather to die in." I was totally taken back. I looked helplessly at him, not knowing what to say, my face laden with surprise.

"He could at least have chosen nice weather to die in don't you think?" he said, his Irish brogue heavier than usual. What surprised me most was he said it loud enough for anyone who cared to to hear.

I regretted then that my parents were such taciturn people. I did not know that my uncles were enemies. Or at least that Uncle Tom hated Uncle Bud. Uncle Bud had lived the last six months of his life with us, and although I don't recall him mentioning Uncle Tom by name, he certainly never said anything unkind about him.

Uncle Tom was above average height, heavily built, with flat iron-grey hair that slid down over his forehead in a sideways V. He wore round glasses in brown tortoiseshell frames. He had a ruddy complexion and a ready smile.

I slipped from beneath his arm, embarrassed beyond words, and headed for the refreshment table. I stuffed myself with chocolate cake while I shrugged off my "ordeal" which was people's favourite word for what I had been through. Every once in a while I would hear Uncle Tom's voice rise above the buzz in conversation, repeating his observation about Uncle Bud not having the decency to die in warm weather.

A few moments later I heard him say, "I expect he's well on his way to hell by now." I didn't turn around to see who he was talking to, but he made the statement matter-of-factly, with just a hint of truculence in his voice, daring anyone to disagree with him. Everyone displayed a great deal of patience with my uncle, including my father who was not known as a patient man. Uncle Tom had come from Nebraska as a young man, come west to be a cowboy, and married my Aunt Lizzie on Valentine's Day, 1907. He was not part of the family, and seemed to me to be asking for trouble. A tiny woman sitting near me on the sofa-couch in the cold living room, a very old woman with a speckled-hen-coloured dress, who smelled of Mentholatum, said quietly, "Tom feels bad too. He just doesn't want anyone to know."

That, I thought, is what must be meant by Christian charity.

In my memory both my uncles are pleasant men, hard-working Irish farmers, genial talkers, good neighbours, infinitely patient with children. It still seems impossible that Uncle Tom could have said the things he did at the after-funeral gathering.

I never quite liked my uncle so much after that day. Three years later he was at our home in the city when my father died. In fact he came to the basement about 5:00 a.m. to wake me. "You'd better come upstairs, Son," he said, touching my arm. "I think your dad is nearing the end."

About five minutes later my father died, a half-dozen of us standing awkwardly around his bed. I remember thinking that when I die, I want to die alone. When I'm ill I'm like an animal that burrows deep into wild grasses. I want to be alone until I either emerge healed, or die. If any act in the world should be private it is death. As soon as his whistling breath had ceased, and my cousin, a retired nurse who had been giving him injections of morphine for over a week, pronounced him dead, my mother put her arm around my waist and said "There are just the two of us now," and we walked down the hall to the kitchen.

Later, in the yard, where sweet peas were strung like a bright, fragrant blanket against the back wall of the house, my uncle tried to offer some consolation.

"Your father was a decent man," he said. "He wasn't one of those foul-mouthed types . . ." and he stopped awkwardly, searching for words, not finding any. All the time he was struggling I wanted very badly to laugh. "At least he died in fine weather," I wanted to say, or, "Would you like to hear a couple of priest and nun jokes?" I insisted on attending school that morning, because I had a final exam to write in Algebra. I didn't tell even my closest friends that my father had died. A few of them read the announcement in the newspaper and came to the funeral.

On the drive home from Uncle Bud's funeral I kept expecting my parents to comment on Uncle Tom's behaviour. But they didn't. My father apologized to me for making us late for the funeral; I think he thought it was some sort of honour for me to be a pallbearer.

"What did they quarrel about?" I wanted to ask. But I knew it must be some adult matter. "It's nothing to concern yourself about," they would have said, if I had asked.

In the days after the funeral I tried to imagine what they could have fallen out about. What could have made Tom hate his brother-in-law so irrationally that even death could not bring forgiveness? Uncle Bud was a lifelong bachelor, he lived his life on a small, rented farm, only about four miles from the original homestead, and only a couple of miles from where Uncle Tom farmed for about forty years. Could the problem have been financial? Bud couldn't have cheated Tom; Uncle Bud owned nothing, while Uncle Tom retired a comfortable, if not wealthy man.

My dad gave Uncle Bud spending money for cigarettes and his prescriptions. In those last months my dad paid Bud's train fare to California, where three of their sisters were settled.

"Bud hasn't seen the girls for over twenty years," he said, in justification of the expense, which he couldn't afford. "Bud's not going to be with us that much longer."

Uncle Bud brought back two photos from California: in one he is standing on an upended orange-crate, in front of an orange-laden tree, three oranges displayed for the camera, held in a triangular shape by his long slim fingers. In the other he is astride a small donkey, his long legs nearly touching the ground. On the back of the photo, in my uncle's shaky handwriting, are the words "Bud sitting on his ass."

As it turned out my father's prophecy was accurate. Uncle Bud had never been sick before. "A heart murmur," was the way both he and my father described his illness. Uncle Bud was over six feet tall, with a long, narrow face, pinched cheeks, and a receding chin. He had been bald for as long as I could remember. His voice was his most unique quality; it was resonant and melodic. Someone described my own reading voice as caramel, and I think I inherited that voice from my uncle. It was only a few days before he died that I realized he had a strong Irish brogue. He telephoned from downtown, I answered, and in that way one has of listening more closely to a voice fed directly into the ear, I became aware of the brogue, and realized that my father spoke in the same manner.

It is curious, but I don't think we ever visited Uncle Bud at his farm. Once or twice a year, whether we lived on a farm or in the city, we visited Uncle Tom and Aunt Lizzie, we visited another uncle who lived in the area, even some cousins, but Uncle Bud always showed up at one relative's or another. I think even at Uncle Tom's, though I can't be certain.

When we visited Uncle Tom on the farm, I would play in the yard, which was about three inches deep in a dark green carpet of creeping charlie, its tiny purple flowers glistening in the dew of morning. The machine shed smelled of grease, grain dust, and chicken droppings. The inside walls of the machine shop were papered with car licence plates, hundreds of them, tacked to the walls with shingle nails. "There's at least one for every year for as long back as there's been licence plates," Uncle Tom declared proudly. The little rectangles were colourful as exotic birds; they were metal with raised numbers and letters, and in one corner the year: 1922, 1923, 1944. I begged a piece of paper from my aunt and with a dull pencil tried to make a list of all the years represented. I was never able to accomplish it, though I don't suppose I tried after I was ten or eleven.

It was Uncle Bud who introduced me to baseball. Not with a ball and bat but with a board-game. As an only child raised, until I was ten, on an isolated farm, I had no opportunity to play baseball, although my father had been a pretty fair semi-pro player in Florida, California, and around the Montana coppermines, and my mother loved to listen to games from St. Louis on our huge battery-powered radio. Uncle Bud arrived at Christmas with a baseball board-game. I was about seven. At first I wanted nothing to do with it, but Uncle Bud, showing great patience, coaxed me into trying it, refusing to play cards, or any of the other games I liked until I agreed. The game was played with dice, a board in the shape of a baseball field, and two teams of markers, one yellow, one green, to use as baseball players. The players were placed on the field, the batting player rolled the dice and moved his men around the bases according to 12-single, 7-double, 2-homerun, 3-walk, 6-strike out, all the rest of the numbers were outs. Not very sophisticated, and we soon abandoned the board and would just roll the dice and mark down the scores. Within a day we had made up a league of real and imagined teams, names culled from an ancient issue of the *St. Louis Sporting News* my father had purchased in the city in the summer. I still remember that my ace pitcher was named Arsenic O'Reilly, and he played for Tyler, Texas, a name I thought quite exotic at the time. Uncle Bud's pitcher was named Hal Eleuah, and he pitched for Mobile, Alabama. I was in high school before I recognized the play on words.

While visiting Uncle Tom I would spend hours bouncing a small red-and-white ball off the side of the machine shed. I kept statistics for whole leagues in my head. I think my mother and aunt worried about me: out while the dew was still on the grass, lingering until it was too dark to see the ball, all day bouncing a rubber ball off a wall, fielding and throwing again.

Uncle Tom offered again and again to take me out on the tractor, the swather or the cultivator.

"No thank you," I said repeatedly. I was scared of the farm machinery, scared of the horses.

"Well, since you play ball, the least I can do is teach you to throw a curveball,'' my uncle said, and brought out his own mitt and a real baseball. Again and again he showed me how to grip the baseball, how to follow through with my body, how to pitch from the stretch. Both he and my father assumed that I bounced the ball off the wall because I lacked companionship. They assumed that because I was alone I was lonely. For me there was no thrill in playing catch. I much preferred my own solitary game, pitting exotic teams and players against each other.

There are so many questions that can never be asked. I wonder if most families are like mine? My own daughters are grown up now, one of them is curious about the past. But I don't answer her questions honestly. I digress, I change the subject, I give veiled answers.

I made a list one day of all the questions I'd like to ask my mother, beginning with ''Was your marriage happy?'' I have never asked any of them, never will.

I phoned my mother last week; she is very old now, and lives in genteel retirement in a highrise in Great Falls, with her younger sister.

Late in the conversation, after we had exhausted our health and the weather I said, ''I've been thinking about Uncle Bud and Uncle Tom. What did they quarrel about? Do you know? Do you remember?''

''It was so long ago,'' my mother said, ''I never knew the whole story, but it was something to do with a baseball.''

There was a long silence at my end.

Something about a baseball!

''I don't remember anything more than that.''

There was another long silence. My mother remembers the record of the Minnesota Twins for every year since they entered the American League; she remembers their won-lost record and who the best players were. She knows more about Harmon Killebrew than she does about me. She remembers her bedroom in Norwich, Connecticut, from when she was two years old. She can describe the ceiling of that bedroom.

''That's all I can remember. Perhaps one of the girls would know. I could ask them.''

"No, don't bother. It was only idle curiosity."

By *the girls* she meant my cousins, Uncle Tom's daughters, who are old women themselves now. I haven't seen any of them for over twenty years.

Something about a baseball! Hearing that was like having a bucket of cold water dashed over my head.

How could it have come about? A souvenir stolen?

I've thought about Bud and Tom many times over the years. I have considered a number of subjects about which they might have quarrelled. But something about a baseball!

Since the quarrel seemed one-sided, I considered that perhaps Uncle Tom knew some terrible secret. It wasn't until I was an adult that I considered there might have been something sexual in the nature of their falling-out. As far as I know, Uncle Bud lived alone all his life. In those days single men were not automatically sexually suspect. Sexual preference or lack of it was never discussed. I managed to graduate from high school without knowing that homosexuality existed.

If I had to guess, I would say that Uncle Bud was probably not homosexual. But what if he was? What if Uncle Tom discovered some liaison or other? What if the unforgivable had happened and Bud made some suggestion, however subtle, or unsubtle? What if out of sheer lonliness he had confessed his secret vice?

The latter would have been enough. The whole family, excepting my father, were straightlaced Irish Catholics, sexually repressed, hypocritical and hysterical in their beliefs. They went to mass at 6:00 a.m. in the freezing old church, they decorated our car with St. Christopher's Medals as we prepared to return home after one of our infrequent visits; at Christmas, Easter, and birthdays they sent garish religious cards stuffed fat with religious pamphlets. I remember cousins, and sisters and aunts, hissing like prostitutes, drawing my father off into one cold parlour or another, to plead with him to return to the church.

Various aunts tried to talk to me of Jesus, when my parents were out of hearing. My defence was to become hyperactive, plead for food, or to play a game, or for a trip to the bathroom.

One of them sent me a cardboard Nativity scene for Christmas, another sent a white-covered Bible.

On the other hand, I considered the possibility that Uncle Tom had done something injurious to Uncle Bud. Cheated him, told lies about him, borne false witness; then unable to accept what he had done, chose to believe the evil he had created.

But, "Something about a baseball!"

After the phone coversation with my mother I went for a walk. Watching the stars, standing with my neck bent back until my vertebrae cracked, staring at the silver-flecked ink of the night, I saw not comets or moons, but baseballs. I saw baseballs arching across the heavens, tumbling with mischief.

I remember, once in my childhood, after an all-night rain, walking to the park behind our house and finding it alive with frogs. The ground was paved with tiny frogs no bigger than nickels. "It rained frogs," a self-assured playmate said. I wanted to credit the phenomenon to some magic gone awry. "Mostly it rains water but sometimes it rains frogs," he said. "A cloud full of frogs passed over us. It don't need to be explained no other way."

Something about a baseball!

I wouldn't want to know the facts now, even if I could. The possibilities of imagination are too wonderful. Two sensible, intelligent men quarrelling with such bitterness over a baseball, that one raged against the other far beyond death, is, indeed stranger than fiction.

I wonder where the baseball is? Rotted back to earth, I suppose. Perhaps stashed safely away by one or the other, lost among the undulating grasses on one farm or another. Ashes to ashes. Bud, dead thirty-five years. Tom dead twenty.

Game called because of darkness.

Nursie

Nursie

"Blood won out," is the first thing Foxy says to me as he comes bounding through the door of our apartment. He takes the living room in two leaps, like he was a big hound dog, and ends up leaning on the narrow counter that's covered in plants and dirty dishes. Nursie and me are at the kitchen table, eating toast, drinking coffee, and arguing. Marty is sitting in his scabby high-chair, dipping his fingers in his porridge and flicking the gooey mess onto the floor. "Blood won out," Foxy says again, grinning lopsidedly. He pushes his long, straight, fox-coloured hair back from his forehead.

"What are you doing up at this god-awful hour?" I say. "I've got an excuse, I gotta catch a plane in an hour." I'm glad Foxy is here, his presence will keep Nursie from snapping at me. It's like she knows I'm going to be gone a while and has to air all her grievances before I get away.

"I gotta say goodbye to my best friend. You can think of me lounging around here for two more weeks . . ." I'm leaving for spring training today. Foxy is in the Yankee organization and doesn't have to report as early as I do.

Nursie is pale and the skin under her eyes is puffy. She has her lank blonde hair pulled into a ponytail and held in place by a pale-green elastic. She takes a sip of her coffee and looks daggers at Foxy, pretending to be offended. Or maybe, this being 6:00 a.m., she really is offended.

Foxy stares back at her, his eyes a wide, innocent green.

I nod my head toward the coffee pot and Foxy gets himself a cup, pours, and doctors. "Yes sir, Angel and I been a little worried for the last week or two. But, as I said . . ."

"We know," says Nursie, "we don't need diagrams."

"What we needed was diaphrams," laughs Foxy, throwing back half his coffee as if it were a shot of whiskey.

"Do you have to be so crude about everything. I'm sure Angella must be thrilled that you're running around town broadcasting the news." Nursie's eyes bore hatefully into Foxy. Angella is Nursie's best friend. "You're wasting yourself on a bum like Foxy," she's told Angella two dozen times in my presence and god knows how many times when they're alone.

"Yeah, don't be so crude, Foxy," I say. "This is raspberry jam I'm eating with my toast."

The force with which Nursie pushes her chair back from the table causes both our cups to slop on the dingy arborite. Marty squawks and raises his sticky hands, but she ignores him and heads for the bedroom, her ratty housecoat billowing a little, showing her white legs. Her slippers slap irritatingly on the linoleum.

"What'd I say wrong?" shrugs Foxy, grinning. "She hates me so much I'd think she'd be happy Angel ain't having my kid."

I remember, must have been five years ago, when we were still in high school, Foxy saying to me, "Nursie really knows how to hate. She has brothers and sisters."

The whole trouble with our marriage may be that I don't know how to hate, or at least how to express it.

I try to talk Foxy into riding to the airport with us. But I can't blame him for not wanting to ride back to town with Nursie, not in the mood she's in.

We fight all the way to the airport. Or she fights and I defend. I'm like a boxer who never attacks, just fends off punches by his opponent. She's being really whiny and unreasonable about my having to leave for spring training. If I've explained once I've explained ten times, I have it right in my contract that I must report to Sun City, Arizona, on February 12th.

"You're in better shape than anybody on the team," says Nursie. She is driving. I'm leaning against the passenger door. Marty is between us, stuffed into his car seat. "You run your five miles every day and you and Foxy use the gym to throw and bat. How come you got to go two months before the season starts and how come Foxy doesn't have to go?" Her voice has a mean whine to it and she twangs out the final word; if it was writing it would take a whole line to itself.

The reason Nursie and me got together was more on account of her than me. I mean I had my eye on a couple of girls: Cassie Hewko, for one. Cassie was tall, with dandelion-coloured hair and the cutest little lower lip I ever seen, so cute I used to dream about kissin' on where it bulged out there, pink and sweet as a baby's finger. Or Angella Quitman, who was Nursie's best girlfriend, even back in high school. Angella printed her name on the back of her denim jacket in a kind of fuschia-coloured ink, only all she printed was Angel, and to me there was something awful sexy about that. Being taller than most, I was able to stare down the hall at high school, over that sea of bobbing heads, and watch the word Angel floating along in the crowd. Angel had long, black hair, with freckles across her nose and on each cheek, and as far down toward her breasts as I could see was the dazzling texture of a speckled bird's egg.

Nursie's real name is Jane-Marie. I've known her all her life. I guess I really took notice of her first back about Grade 7. She had white, white blonde hair. Even then her face was too long, her nose too big, and her lips sealed up tight like she knew too many secrets. Her dad worked in the railroad yards, a big man with a flour-sack belly pushing against the front of his striped overalls. Her mom had been a nurse, but went off to visit her sister in Lexington and got run over by a taxi right in front of the railroad station. She left behind a whole closetful of nurse uniforms, and Jane-Marie's daddy figured it was wasteful not to make use of them, so he made Jane-Marie wear them to school, made her wear the white nurse-shoes too. Jane-Marie, always pale as death, her face peaked and her lips sealed up, looked like a ghost as she walked around the school. The only real colour about her was on one shoulder of them dresses, I can never remember which, but there was a red cross the dark colour of blood. The kids used to call her Nursie, and at noon hour some guys would pretend to faint, or to have broken arms or legs, and call for a nurse. But it wasn't a fun kind of teasing and Nursie knew that. It was teasing that let her know she was different.

I've known since I was about nine years old that I was going to make it to the Bigs. I figure I've got two more years to go. After spring training I'm betting I'll be assigned to a Class A team. Next year I'll get a tryout with whatever big-league team owns my contract; I won't make it, but I'll be assigned to a Triple A, and two years from now I'll be in the Bigs. Three years from now I'll be a regular starter. I mean I've planned it all, right from the time I went to the St. Louis Cardinal tryout camp. Foxy got drafted by the Yankees out of Iowa; he was about 95th and didn't even get his name in the *Des Moines Register*. He was 12-4 in the rookie league last year; he'll hit the Bigs the same time as me.

"Maybe what'll happen, what I hope'll happen," I tell Nursie as we drive, "is that the San Francisco Giants will buy my contract, then I'll get to play in Cedar Rapids. That way I'll be able to live at home half the summer. Wouldn't that be great?"

"You got a hell of an imagination," says Nursie. Then, "Wipe the kid's face." I look at Marty and he's drooling from teething and his face looks like he's been eating licorice. I remember the time in high school we got scouted by the Cubs. Onamata was up against West High from Iowa City, and they were the strongest team in Double A High School in the state. The day of the game I was so choked up with a cold I felt like my mouth and nose were stuffed with warm flannel. I went 1/5, we lost the game 8-2, and one time I threw to the wrong base. The old scout from the Cubs sat in a bleacher on the first base side, chewed a cigar and made notes in a black binder. I figured sure I'd be drafted out of college, and even when I wasn't it never occurred to me to give up. I used the last of our savings to take the bus to Florida to the Cardinal tryout camp. I knew that only two or three of the 200 players there would make it, but I knew I'd be one of them. And I was.

"I'd think you'd be ashamed," says Nursie, "goin' off and leavin' your family in a mess like we're in. You should get a regular job."

She's only saying that to hurt me, I tell myself. Ignore it, in half an hour I'll be on the plane. I mean, some of what she says is right. We've got it rough financially. We never intended for Nursie to get pregnant with Marty, or with the one she's carrying. But it ain't just me that's to blame.

I guess I'll never understand about families, and brothers and sisters, about fighting and forgiving. I'm an only child. My dad worked in an office for Proctor and Gamble, in Iowa City; my mother taught kindergarten, right here in Onamata. My parents never fought; they used to snap at each other if they were tired, but they never really fought, or said hurtful things that couldn't be forgiven. And I don't either. I try to reason things out. Some families, it seems to me, fight for pure enjoyment. Nursie's family is like that. Her and her brothers and sister Barbara will stand nose to nose, like an umpire and a manager, and yell curses and insults into each other's faces. Ten minutes later they'll be laughing and joking as if nothing had happened, as if they weren't enemies anymore.

Nursie and I been going together since we were about fifteen. Sometimes I wouldn't call around on her for a month or two; I'd chase after the girls I thought were pretty or sexy, or maybe just because they were known to put out. Nursie, when I got around to calling on her, was always sort of grateful. I liked that. And I liked the way she was always there. She'd be glad to see me and she'd figure a way for us to be alone, even if it was to take me into her bedroom. The house Nursie lived in was kind of a converted garage, in fact it was an abandoned Amoco station. Her old man hauled in some partitions from some other abandoned building and none of them reached to the ceiling. Nursie's house was like some offices I been in — if you tried really hard you could look into any room in the house at any time, even the washroom. Nursie had five little brothers who swung like monkeys from room to room. But Nursie would hang onto my arm like she was scared and she'd take me straight into her bedroom, looking right at her old man, if he was home, her eyelids drooped down, daring him to say something to her or to me.

"Jimmy and me got some private talking to do," she'd say, leading me into her room where she'd fling her arms around my neck and kiss me so sweet, her tongue just walking around inside my mouth. We'd lie beside each other and rub together, but never do more than that because of the way the house was set up. If Nursie was feeling in a particularly good mood she'd let me slip my hand down inside her jeans and feel the silky hair and the slick wetness of her. In the next room her brothers would fight, curse, throw punches, the loser would cry for a while and then they'd begin again. Once, Nursie spotted one hanging like a cat, peering over the partition. She grabbed a shoe and smashed his fingers until he let go. He screamed for half an hour. But as I was leaving he was hugging Nursie while she mussed his hair and kissed him a couple of times.

Once, in college, after me and Foxy had been off to Minneapolis for a few days, catching a few Twins' games, when I came to call on Nursie she met me at the door and said why didn't we go walking for a while. She was skittish and wouldn't let me kiss her or hardly even hold her hand. I guess she was expectin' that I brought her a present of some kind. But I hadn't. The hotel cost more than we'd expected, and me and Foxy had gone out on the town a time or two.

The weather was cloudy and the air was thick and sweet with the odour of lilac. I finally grabbed Nursie, turned her toward me and kissed her. But even that didn't please her. She kept pulling away, made her lips thin, and kept her teeth closed tight. When I let her loose she said under her breath but loud enough for me to hear, "Mouthful of rotten teeth," and she turned her back on me.

I'd never say anything like that to Nursie, or to anybody, even if it was true. I couldn't say something like that to somebody I loved. If I wanted to hurt somebody that badly I wouldn't ever want to have anything to do with them again. I knew what she said wasn't true. I've never had a cavity in my mouth and I brush my teeth until they're white as new baseballs. I knew she was only saying it to hurt me, and that I ought to say something back, but I couldn't. But I also knew I'd never kiss her again in my life but what I'd think of what she said. After Nursie and her family boiled over at each other, they'd seem to love each other again, almost right away. I always think before I speak. I don't say things I don't mean and I expect other people to do the same.

I stayed away from Nursie for most of a month. I even dated a cheerleader who looked like a movie star and gave a whole new meaning to corn fed. But she liked to dip herself in perfume and she kissed kind of half-heartedly without taking the gum out of her mouth. Nursie always had only her own sweet odours about her.

"I ain't seen you for a while," she said when I called on her again. It was just as if nothing had happened. "I'm real glad you come by, Jimmy. I thought maybe you was mad at me."

"Nah," I said.

"Well I missed you, I did. I get awful blue when you don't come around. You know that, don't you?"

"I know," I said.

We went out and sat on the wooden swing in her back yard. She lifted her legs up over mine and started kissing on me like I was a piece of raw meat and she been starved for a month.

"Jane-Marie, honey," I said, using her real name for first time in years, "I think you and me ought to get married. I'm crazy for you, honey, and I do love you." Nursie was so soft and warm in my arms. I did love her. I do love her.

Nursie said yes so fast I hardly knew what happened.

"If we go for the blood test tomorrow we can get married on Saturday," she said, and I didn't have the heart to tell her I hadn't expected us to move quite so fast. But she didn't object when I suggested we walk over to Foxy's apartment. I knew he was up at Cedar Rapids watching a ballgame and wouldn't be home until late.

The first time we made love was in the back of Foxy's car at the drive-in near Cedar Rapids. We just got to a certain point and from there on Nursie wouldn't let me stop. She was pulling off her clothes and mine at the same time and an earthquake couldn't have stopped us. I suppose the fact that Foxy and Angella Quitman were in the front seat and getting it on so loud and wild that I thought sure they'd shake the seat off its hinges or whatever holds car seats in place, had something to do with exciting us. One night Foxy or Angella knocked the car out of gear and we rolled back down into the lane between the rows of speakers. Foxy never stopped what he was doing for a second and I couldn't reach the brake from the back seat. I just watched as the car rolled real slow and the speaker cord stretched tighter and tighter, the big microphone-shaped speaker crushed against the window. Finally the cord broke and the speaker smashed against Foxy's back, and he yelled and was gonna blame it on me until I pointed out where we were.

And I remember back in grade school, Nursie, pale as snow in her white uniform and shoes, and us guys yelling, "Hey, Nursie, we got something to show you. We got something over here needs nursing," and we'd all laugh like maniacs.

All the way to the airport Nursie has been mad as hell. She knows all the whys and wherefors of what I have to do but she's still ticked off. In some ways I can't blame her. As she drives, the goddamn old Dodge coughs and creaks and we can smell exhaust fumes and feel the heat of the engine. "Two more years and I'll be making good money," I've told her a dozen times, while we looked at new cars in showrooms in Iowa City. I mean Nursie's never had a thing in her life and it doesn't seem too much to ask for her to wait another year or two for the good things to start rolling in. I don't mean that I'm such a terrific catch and all, but my family's always had a good home and never lacked for necessities. "Beer and hard times," is how people talked about Nursie's family. "You can't expect much from a house where there's no mother and a father that drinks." One of Nursie's brothers works as a labourer in Iowa City and drinks like his old man; another one's in jail for stealing cars; her big sister worked at K-Mart in the lunch counter until she married a stockboy who came from Pakistan. He got transferred to Tulsa, Oklahoma, and we ain't heard from them for two years.

I take Marty out of his car seat. He laughs as I pull him up until he's standing stiff-legged. He hangs on tight to each of my thumbs and grins like an idiot, showing his few teeth.

We've had a couple of rough years. Rookie League didn't pay enough for us to live on. I was gone from February to Labour Day. Baseball clubs move their minor-league players around the country as if the owners were kids playing marbles. Last year my contract was sold to the Butte Copper Kings. We spent most of the summer riding a bus across Montana and Alberta. We played teams from Helena, Calgary, Lethbridge, and Medicine Hat. I had to send home pictures; Nursie didn't believe there was a place called Medicine Hat.

I guess I've always expected Nursie to be a little more proud of me than she is. I guess she can't see the future the way I can. I don't think she really believes I'm gonna make the Bigs. I admit she's got it rough. But there ain't much can be done about it right now. I don't even blame her for being ticked off, but it seems to me this is a time when we should stick together, a time when we should touch a lot cause we won't be touching but by letter and once in a while by phone.

"I sure do get blue when you're away from me," Nursie says when her mood is good, and comes and sits in my lap. Sometimes I think she'd rather have a man like her father, who never provided decently for his family but was always around, warm and hairy as a big dog.

I always sleep poorly when I know I have to get up early, and this morning I been awake since before daylight. When I heard Marty stirring I got up and fixed him a bottle and changed his pants, putting baby powder on his bum and scattering more in the air, like incense, to kill the ammonia odour. But when I got back to bed Nursie made herself all stiff as a piece of lumber when I pulled her against me. After a minute, when I could tell she wasn't going to be friendly, I shoved off to my own side of the bed.

"You didn't get the TV set fixed," Nursie says. She has been lining up grievances all the way from Onamata, hurrying

them, throwing them up at me urgently as if time will run out
before she can let me know everything that is bothering her.

"I don't have the money," I say, freeing one hand from
Marty's grip so I can gesture helplessly. In the off season I wait
on tables at a restaurant called Iowa Light and Power Company, not regularly, just when they need me. I don't make
much money. "Look, I've arranged for the club to send you all
but fifty dollars a month of my cheque. It will be deposited to
our account. Maybe *you* can manage it better than I can.
Maybe *you* can afford to fix the TV."

"I could fix it if there was enough money. You just don't
provide . . ."

I don't say anything. I want to tell her that as bad as I do,
she's better off than she ever was with her father. Instead I say,
"You knew I was a ballplayer when you married me. You
didn't complain when I proposed . . ."

"Yeah, well you liked me better then," she says, making her
lips thin, her way of pouting.

"I like you as well as I ever did," I say. "It's your imagination, like this morning . . ."

"Oh, that," she says. For a minute I think she's about to
apologize, something that could be a smile twitches at the corner of her mouth, but then her face becomes rigid again.

"It's gonna be at least four months before you see me again
. . ." I say.

"I'm glad you're gonna be gone," says Nursie. "I won't
have to put up with your pawing me." She stares at me, her
hazel eyes dead as wood chips. "You aren't half as good as you
think you are."

I mean if I was ever to hit a woman, this would be the time.
But I don't. I don't say anything. We are silent right until she
stops the car in the circle driveway in front of Cedar Rapids
Airport. I know she didn't mean what she said, but deep down
it hurts as bad as if she did. When Nursie ain't in a bad mood
we do take on with one another, and don't Nursie like it
though. But now her words hang in the air like a mean shadow.

"You're lucky," Nursie said to Angella just the other day,
"you can walk away from Foxy any time, and you should." I
was looking across the table at Angella, watching her full, sen-

sual lips, her tongue pink as strawberries brushing her lips repeatedly as she spoke. I tried to imagine what it would be like
to make love to her, tried to imagine why I chose Nursie when I
probably could have had Angella, tried to define why Nursie,
pale and plain as she is, makes my stomach flop and my chest
tighten when I look at her.

As Nursie stops the car I put Marty back in his car seat. I
kiss his cheeks and he giggles real pretty. I shake his dimpled
little hand and say, "Take care of your mama."

I walk around the car and take my duffel bag and suitcase
from the trunk. It takes about ten tries to get that bunged-up
old trunk lid to close. I was gonna walk right into the airport,
but I just couldn't. Instead I go around to the driver's window,
jingling my keys.

"Guess I won't need these on the road," I say, and hand
them to her. Nursie is lookin' straight ahead. "You take care
now," I say.

I lean in to kiss her cheek, only she turns toward me just as I
do, and our lips kind of brush.

"You too," she says, and I catch the smell of her that I love,
that kind of new-rope smell that is hers all alone, and I feel so
lonesome all of a sudden, right down deep in my gut that I just
about grab her and cover her with kisses.

Instead I grab up my bags and wrestle them through the
doors into the airport.

I'm able to check my luggage right through to Arizona,
though I'm gonna have to change planes three times. I have
over an hour to kill. The Cedar Rapids Airport is small. I can
walk from one end to the other in less than a minute. I stare at
the rows of men in business suits, sitting red-eyed, hugging
briefcases. I sit on a red upholstered stool in the coffee shop,
order coffee, drink about half of it. I stare out of the window to
the tarmac where the green-and-white Ozark Airlines plane is
being serviced. Finally I stop in front of a scrawny little
machine that sells flight insurance. The top isn't much bigger
than an old-fashioned parking meter. A round, black pole runs
down about two feet and disappears into a black, dome-shaped
box with something that resembles a mail-slot in it. Funny-
looking business, I think, a black igloo with a slot in its face,

and a parking meter protruding from the top. *Mutual of Omaha* is printed in green letters across the parking meter.

I guess what makes me read all the instructions for buying flight insurance is that I am feeling a little sorry for Nursie. She's on her way back home to our crumby little apartment, Marty gurgling in the car seat, the old car smelling of dust and exhaust fumes. I wish I could fight with her. Is there something wrong with me that I can't go saying terrible things I don't mean to someone I really love? For a minute, as I read the instructions again, I almost blame myself for not being able to be nasty.

I take out some change, play it into the machine, and out comes a little package. Besides about a ton of insurance talk there is a small postcard. I lay it on the top of the machine, fill most of it out, and sign it.

When I get to the line that says *Beneficiary's Name*, I get an idea that downright tickles me. I mean, what could I do that would make Nursie the maddest? What if my plane was to crash and I had lots of insurance, but not made out to her?

I have to go to one of the car rental booths before I can find an Iowa City telephone book. When I find the address, I write it down real carefully on the line beneath *Beneficiary's Name*. When it's all finished it reads: Angella Quitman, 422 North Linn St., Iowa City, Iowa, 52240. I almost howl as I do that. Let Nursie explain that to her no-account family. Let Angella explain it. I wonder how long they'll stay friends. I fill each policy out and plunge each card into the slot in the black igloo. I go over to the coffee shop and get some more change. I punch the coins into the machine and it spits out a new policy each time I do, until I have about $200,000 worth.

In red letters on the front of each policy it says, "Place policy in envelope and mail or give to your beneficiary before flight time." I study the envelope a long time. I could send it all to Angella. Or better still, I could send it to Nursie, all filled out with Angella's name — that would hurt as bad as anything she ever said to me. But no, there ain't no reason for anyone but me to ever know, unless the plane goes down.

The Night Manny Mota
Tied the Record

The Night Manny Mota
Tied the Record

August 7, 1979: Dodger Stadium, Los Angeles, California.
Dodgers are playing Houston Astros. I am seated high above
the field, just to the third-base side of home plate. Pregame
presentations are being made. It is Mormon Family Night.
The stadium is nearly full. It is five days since Thurman Munson died.

I spend my time people-watching. In front of me are a
number of co-workers from an office of some kind, probably a
food company, I decide, noting the size of the women. Every
one of them is overweight, the one directly in front of me by
about two hundred pounds. These women cram their sweating
faces with every variety of concession food. The one in front of
me has purchased a tray of six hotdogs. Several of them have
whole trays of beer, six cups, each slopping foam over its waxy
edge.

To my left, I watch an old man standing in the aisle staring
at his ticket as if trying to decide where his seat should be.
Eventually he chooses my aisle and makes his way to the seat
next to me. He looks like a retired bank manager: iron-grey
hair carefully styled, a blue pin-stripe suit, vest, and tie. He

carries a zippered leather binder. What fascinates me is the ticket he holds in his left hand. As he stands in the aisle it appears to blink like a tiny computer making calculations. It flashes all the way down the row of seats, stopping as he slides into the chair next to mine.

Our eyes meet as he adjusts the small brown leather case in his lap, and I can see the same sense of tragedy floating in his eyes as I have viewed on my own the past five mornings.

"A terrible thing," I say.

He nods gravely. "Did you watch the funeral coverage on TV?"

It is my turn to nod. He has a sincere, fatherly voice that, my mind being preoccupied with the death of Thurman Munson, reminds me of the unseen baseball executive who talks to Munson in a widely shown commercial for a shaving product.

In the commercial, Munson knocks, then enters the executive's office, saying, "What's the problem? I'm playing good ball."

"You certainly are," the unseen executive says. "In my opinion, Thurman Munson is the finest catcher in the game."

As if reading my mind, the dapper old man beside me looks straight into my face and says, "Yes, a terrible loss, to the game and to the fans. In my opinion, Thurman Munson *is* the finest catcher in the game."

I feel like an egg with a finger-painted happy-face on it as I register my surprise.

"Is?" I say.

He leans towards me, smiling wryly, and speaks in a confidential manner. "Death," he says, "need not be as final as many of us are used to believing."

We are interrupted by the playing of the National Anthem. The old man stands at attention with his right hand over his heart. I look around me: everything appears to be normal, the palm trees beyond the left-field fence sway ever so slightly. I can discern nothing out of the ordinary except the presence next to me. When the anthem finishes I remain silent; whatever kind of game we are playing, it is his move.

"What would you say," the old man continues, "if I told

you that it might just be possible to move time back, like a newsreel being played in reverse, and undo what has been done?" He stares at me, half smiling, giving me the chance to joke his statement away if I choose.

"You're talking about Thurman Munson?"

"More or less."

"Are you suggesting that if time were turned back, Munson's plane would have landed safely at the Canton Airport last week? That none of this would have happened?"

He nods.

"But at what price?" I say. "There has to be a catch."

"You're right, of course. As they say, there is no free lunch." He looks long at me, his kindly grey eyes on my face, and I'm sure at that instant we recognize each other for what we are, above and beyond business, family, or religion — baseball fans. The true word is fanciers. Fans of the game itself. Men having favourites, but not blind prejudices, here because we love the game. Not Sunday fathers dragging young sons after us, or college kids guzzling beer and cheering ourselves hoarse, but steady, long-term, win-or-lose fans. I can tell by looking at him that he has seen Mike Marshall work on a sleety April night in Bloomington; that he has endured the arctic cross-winds of Candlestick Park in San Francisco and Exhibition Stadium in Toronto; that he has been jellied in his seat by the steam-cabinet humidity of Busch Stadium in August. I feel towards that old man the camaraderie that soldiers must feel for their fellows as they travel home after a long campaign.

"My name is Revere," he says, extending a manicured hand that is solid as a ham, a baseball player's hand. "I caught a little myself at one time," he says, knowing I can feel the outsize fingers, like plump, scarred sausage. "I think we should have a serious talk."

"The price," I say. "What is the price of tampering with time?"

The game had begun. Jerry Reuss, pitching for the Dodgers, set Houston down in the first without a murmur.

"I'll explain the situation to you exactly as it is. No deception. I'll always be candid with you. Don't feel badly if you don't believe me. In fact, most people don't.''

"Go on," I say.

He talks for a full inning. Explaining to me as if I were a child attending his first baseball game and he were a benevolent grandfather outlining the rules between hotdogs and orange drinks.

"What you're saying is . . . ." but I am interrupted by the rising roar of the crowd as Joe Ferguson of the Dodgers strokes a home run to right field. I was not involved with what was happening and have to stare around the buffalo-like woman in front of me to see if there are runners on base. Revere and I applaud politely, sit down while the people around us are still standing; it is like sliding into the shade of a fence on a summer's day. As the buzz of the crowd subsides I continue:

"What you're saying is that everyone has someone, somewhere, who if contacted and agreeable, could replace them in death."

"Badly put but basically accurate," says Mr Revere. "Limited, of course, to people who have achieved fame or made an outstanding contribution to society, and who still have an outstanding contribution left to make if given a second chance."

"And you're suggesting to me that I might be able to sacrifice myself in order to give Thurman Munson a longer life."

"At this point I am only acquainting you with the situation. I want to make that very clear. There are many of us at locations throughout the world. Our search is rather like a game: we have a few days to find the one person in the world who can, if he or she desires, make the event — in this case Thurman Munson's death — unhappen, so to speak. Experience teaches us that the natural places to be looking are ballparks, taverns, and assembly lines . . ."

"My case would be a little different," I say. "It would be like a chain of command, if I replaced Munson why there would be someone out there who could, if you found him, replace me."

"I'm afraid I don't understand," Mr Revere says, looking

genuinely puzzled.

I introduce myself. "I'm a writer," I say. "I've published four books. Have dozens left to write."

"Really?"

"Short stories, too. Over a hundred of them. I've had very good reviews."

"It's embarrassing," Mr Revere says, "but I would have known if you were on the protected list. Something we never do is ask one protected person to replace another. And it isn't like we didn't know your name. We have ways of knowing things like that," and he taps the side pocket of his suit where he had deposited what may or may not have been a ticket stub that winked and blinked.

"But I'm relatively famous," I protest. "I've made a contribution. I'm at least well known." Mr Revere remains silent. "I *do* have a following."

"I'm sure you do. But you must understand, our list is small. Few writers." He smiles as if reminiscing. "Hemingway was there."

"But you couldn't find his . . ."

"Oh, but we did. Even as a young man he contemplated suicide. Used his service revolver one night. There was a retired bullfighter who replaced him."

Houston goes scoreless in the third. There are a couple of hits but I scarcely notice. Usually I keep a score card. Use a green or purple felt pen and have the card woven over with patterns as if it were a square of afghan. Tonight my program lays whitely on my knee.

"If you're totally appalled at the idea, you must let me know," says Mr Revere. "If you feel that I'm senile, or crazy, or if you know that you could never do such a thing, don't take up my time. There was a certain magic about you or I wouldn't be here."

Thurman Munson: I have never been a fan of his, though I recognized his greatness. It was the Yankees. They have always been like the rich kid on the block who could afford real baseballs and a bat that wasn't cracked. You played him, you tolerated him, but you were never sorry when he got spiked.

"No," I hear myself saying, "tell me more. Still, dying . . ."

"Ceasing to exist," corrects Mr Revere.

"Dying," I insist. "Euphemisms don't change the nature of the beast. It is definitely, ah, quite final?" I ask.

"I'm afraid it would be, as we say, terminal."

Mr Revere settles back to watch the game, a rather sly smile playing at the corners of his mouth.

Ferguson and Yeager hit back-to-back homers for the Dodgers in the fourth. The fans in front of us, whom I have mentally named the Buffalo Brigade, all stand, blocking my vision. The largest woman has made two trips to the concession since the game started. She applauds with half a hotdog protruding obscenely from her mouth. I remain in my seat as each of the home-run hitters circles the bases.

Die. The word rings through me as if it were a bolt rattling in my hollow metal interior. Who would I die for? My wife? I like to think that we are beyond that kind of emotional self-sacrifice. I would, in a split-second situation, endanger myself, say, to push her from the path of a speeding car, but, given a thoughtful choice like this, of quietly dying so the other might live, I suspect we might each choose to save ourselves. My daughters? Yes. In effect I would be saving my own life by saving them. My grandchildren? The blood ties thin. I think not. Is there anyone else? I have never had a friend for whom I would even consider such a sacrifice. A stranger? As unlikely as it seems, there are probably several.

I look over at Mr Revere; he appears engrossed in the game. "Take your time," he says, still looking at the emerald infield. "Feel free to ask questions."

What would motivate someone to make the supreme sacrifice so that a stranger might live? Heroism is the only word I can muster. Heroism, I believe, is something basic to human nature. I have often fantasized delivering my wife or daughters from some holocaust, or walking steely-eyed into the jaws of death to rescue one or more of them, perhaps, afterwards, expiring in their grateful arms, my mission accomplished, the cheers of the crowd fading slowly as my life ebbed.

An idea begins to form. I inch forward on my seat.

"I'm afraid not," Mr Revere says. I look at him harshly.

"Couldn't I rescue him from the plane?" I suggest.

I could see myself racing across the tarmac of that airport near Canton, Ohio, tearing open the door of the plane and dragging Thurman Munson's body to safety, gripping him under the arms like a two-hundred-and-twenty-five-pound sack of flour and backing away from the flaming wreckage. Later, when I was interviewed by television and newspaper reporters, I would speak modestly of my accomplishment, displaying my bandaged hands. I would be known as The Man Who Rescued Thurman Munson.

"Our operatives are always quite anonymous," says Mr Revere.

"No possibility of recognition. It makes the choice harder," I say.

"It eliminates the insincere," says Mr Revere, returning his attention to the game.

I am silent for a few moments. "What would happen to me?" I say to Mr Revere's neatly trimmed, white, right sideburn. He is intent on the game; Houston has a bit of a rally going.

"You needn't have any fear of pain," he replies, sounding, I think, suspiciously like a dentist. "You might, after the game, decide to sleep for a few moments in your car before driving home. It would be peaceful, like sinking into a warm comforter."

"What guarantee do I have?"

"None at all. You would have to sense that I'm telling the truth. You would have to feel the magic, see the world from a slightly different angle, like batting while lying prone."

"Who have you saved? How many?"

"Not as many as we'd like. Our business can be compared to searching for the proverbial needle in the haystack. We have many more failures than successes. The rather sad fact is that no one ever hears of our successes."

"Who?" I insist. "Name names."

He unzippers the leather binder in his lap and produces a front page from the *New York Times*. The headline reads: PRESI-

DENT FORD ASSASSINATED IN SACRAMENTO. Below it is a large photograph of Squeaky Fromme holding a smoking gun.

"We went through four hectic days in 1975, the days after Miss Fromme's gun didn't misfire. Gerald Ford's body was lying in state in Washington when we found the party."

"Of course, there is no way to verify that!"

"Absolutely none." Enos Cabell ends the Astros' fifth but not before they score two runs to cut the Dodger lead to 4-2.

"What about John Kennedy?" I cry. "Half the world would have given their lives for him. I would have. Still would . . ."

"There is only one chance for each person on our list. We saved him once, during the PT-109 sinking. It was a young black woman from Memphis who . . ." and his voice trails off.

I think about Thurman Munson, remember how I heard of his death. I didn't listen to TV or radio the night of August second. Mornings I write. My wife, who teaches at a nearby university, brings a newspaper home at lunchtime. On August third she brought me ice cream to soften the blow. When I'm troubled or disturbed or can't write, I often head for the nearest Baskin-Robbins. At noon on August third, my wife walked into my study without knocking and handed me a cardboard cup overflowing with chocolate and coconut ice cream, my favourites. There was a fuchsia-coloured plastic spoon stabbed into the middle of it.

"There's bad news in the paper," she said.

"Did the Twins lose again?" I replied.

"I'm serious," she added.

I was going to say, "So am I," but didn't as I caught the inflection in her voice.

"Bobby Kennedy?" I say to Mr Revere. "Martin Luther King?"

The Houston Astros, as ragtag a crew of ballplayers as ever held first place in August, are running wild in the sixth inning, forcing errors, blooping hits, stealing bases. In front of us, the Buffalo Brigade are shuffling in and out with new armloads of food. It is very difficult for two fat people to pass in the narrow space between rows.

"We should be thankful they are sitting in front of us rather than behind," says Mr Revere. "If one of them should fall forward, I'm afraid it could be fatal."

I repeat my previous question.

"We were unable to find the party representing Dr King."

"Then he's still out there. You could still . . ."

"We have only a short period. Even now the time for Mr Munson runs low. We did find the man representing Robert Kennedy. In fact I found him myself. He was an Eastern philosopher, a man of great religious piety. He refused to cooperate. He had no qualms about his own fate, but his belief was that death is the highest attainable state; therefore he felt it would be a tremendous disservice to bring any man back to this world after he had experienced the next."

"How do the people feel who come back?"

"They never know they've been away," Mr Revere says. "Gerald Ford thinks that Miss Fromme's gun misfired. Hemingway thought he changed his mind about suicide in 1918. We are able to be of service sometimes, but our odds of success are rather like hitting eighteen in blackjack. Not very high."

"Who is the 'We' you keep referring to? You make it sound like a corporation. Who are you?"

"Perhaps we should watch the baseball game for a while," suggests Mr Revere, smiling kindly.

I look at the scoreboard. The Astros have put up six runs in the sixth inning with my hardly noticing, and now lead 8-4.

I wonder about Thurman Munson. Would he want to come back? I picture Thurman Munson dead, his spine splintered like a bat hit on the trademark. Tentative cause of death, asphyxiation, caused by breathing in toxic chemicals from the burning craft. I understand now why I couldn't be rescuer, why his friends couldn't move his body from the wreckage. His spine shattered; he wouldn't have wanted to be rescued. Would he want to come back now? For all his short life he did what he loved best. He died with the smell of the grass still in his nostrils. The crack of the bat and the rising roar of the crowd never had to fade away and become muted memories like distant thunder. He never lived to hear some fresh kid say, "Who was Thurman Munson?" He left a beautiful wife and a

young family he loved very much. I suppose that would be the
best argument for granting him a second chance, and I recall a
picture in the newspaper of his young son, Michael, wearing a
baseball uniform with Munson's number fifteen, and the story
of his asking why everyone was sad and saying that they should
be happy that Munson was with God. "God has taken Daddy
to heaven because He needs good people there."

Still, I wonder, would that be such a bad way to remember
your father . . . having him taken when you were still young
enough not to realize that he was only a very ordinary mortal?

Some athletes can't adjust to retirement; relationships
disintegrate. There are many old baseball players who sell cars
or insurance, drink too much, and wish that they had gone out
in their prime while they were still adored by the fans. I recall
the emotionally exhausting scene at Yankee Stadium as the
crowd cheered for nine minutes when Thurman Munson's picture was flashed on the scoreboard. Many fans, tears streaming
down their cheeks, cheered themselves into exhaustion,
somehow exorcising the grief that hung in their chests like concrete.

Perhaps, I consider, no one is meant to tamper with time.

I try to concentrate on the game but can't.

"There is magic," Mr Revere says. "It is close by. I can tell
when someone feels it."

"It is the game," I say. "Not you."

"We all have to claim some game as magic," he says and
takes from the inside pocket of his jacket a thick sheaf of paper
that looks like a half-dozen sheets of foolscap folded over. I
strain to get a look at what is written on them. I can't
distinguish the letterhead, but there appears to be long lists of
questions with little boxes after each, places for Mr Revere to
make X's or check marks.

"Name?" and he reads my full name for me to verify. "A
writer, you say. I'm afraid I haven't read anything of yours.
My job keeps me quite busy, as you can imagine."

During the next inning Mr Revere plies me with more irrele-
vant questions than a tax return and loan application combined. There are questions about ancestry, employment, fam-

ily, hobbies; it is as though I am being interviewed by a very thorough reporter. I am reminded that I once underwent, in connection with an employment application, the MMPI (Minnesota Multiphasic Personality Inventory), a series of several hundred questions designed to supply a detailed personality profile. Mr Revere's questions are equally probing but do not include such MMPI gems as: *Are you a messenger of God?* and *Has your pet died recently?*

As I answer the questions my mind is working at three levels, with the baseball game being relegated to the lowest, Mr Revere's questions to the second level, while my top priority becomes: What will I do if I am chosen?

I am forty-eight years old; I am not ready to die.

"Thurman Munson was only thirty-two and he wasn't ready to die either," says Mr Revere between questions.

In my time, given this opportunity, who would I die for? The names flash past me like calendar pages blown in the wind: FDR, Dr Tom Dooley, Bobby Greenlease, Perry Smith, Bogart, Jim Reeves, Elvis, Lyman Bostock, Martin Luther King, Gandhi, James Dean, Amelia Earhart, Lou Gehrig . . .

"Given the choice, would you rather be an aeronautical engineer, a sign painter, or a dishwasher?"

My head feels as though a dealer is shuffling cards inside it, his thumbs have slipped, and I'm inundated in an avalanche of playing cards. "What on earth do you care for? I have zero mechanical ability. I can't draw. I would rather be a dishwasher."

"I'm sorry," Mr Revere says, giving me his grandfatherly smile. "Everything used to be much simpler. We are experimenting with some rather advanced concepts in hopes of increasing our success rate. I'm sure you understand."

I recall Sidney Carton's words from *A Tale of Two Cities*, something to the effect that " 'Tis a far, far better thing I do than ever I have done before." It is only the hero complex again, rising out of the crowd in front of me like the Loch Ness monster.

"Why me?" I almost shout, causing several people to glance my way briefly, annoyed that I have distracted them from the excitement of a Dodger rally in the eighth.

"Because you love the game for the sake of the game. There aren't many of us left. It is rather like finding a genuinely religious person . . ."

"I'm not exactly unprejudiced," I say. "To put it mildly, I have never been a Yankee fan. I resent a team that buys its winning percentage."

"You disapprove of the management, but do you hate the players?"

"Hate is a word that has no place in sports. I've never cheered for Thurman Munson, except in all-star games, but I don't hang over railings with a red face and hair in my eyes screaming insults either."

"And you stay until the last out, even if one team is winning 12-0." I nod. But the question remains: What will I do if he chooses me? I feel like the thirteenth at table. A chance to be either a god or a devil.

The crowd suddenly breaks into a chant: "Manny! Manny! Manny!" Rhythmic, ritualistic, the voice of the crowd rises like a monstrous choir as the leather-faced veteran Manny Mota appears from the dugout to swing his bat in the on-deck circle.

Manny Mota has 143 pinch hits in his career and needs one to tie and two to break the record held by Smoky Burgess.

"Manny! Manny! Manny!" the crowd rhapsodizes as he approaches the plate.

The largest of the Buffalo Brigade, built to resemble a chest of drawers with an encyclopaedia set on top of it, stunned by copious amounts of beer, remains standing even after Mota has stepped into the batter's box, completely blocking my view. Shouts of "Down in front," come from other people whose view is also obstructed. She ignores the shouts, if she hears them. She stands sturdy and dark as a pillar, a container of beer raised in her cupcake hand.

On a two-strike count Mota slashes a hard grounder to the right side. Landestoy, the Houston second baseman, gets in front of it, but the force of the ball turns him around. He regains his balance and fires to first but the split-second delay was all Mota needed: he is safe on a very close play. The fans roar their approval. Mota tips his hat to the crowd. When he is replaced by a pinch runner the crowd stands again to cheer him back to the dugout.

Mr Revere, apparently through with his interrogation, folds the legal-size pages of questions and, unzipping his leather binder, places them carefully in the bottom between what look like sheets of cardboard or black plastic that may have been blinking golden like a night sky.

The briefcase seems to be making a whirring sound as if thousands and thousands of tiny impulses are perhaps processing the information just fed to it.

I look around at the ecstatic crowd. I look at the fat lady, still standing.

"I've decided to do it," I say to Mr Revere.

"I know," and he smiles in his most kindly manner and I somehow picture a sweet-pea- and petunia-scented evening on the veranda of a square, white, two-storey house somewhere in Middle America where a grandfather and a child sit in the luminous dusk and talk of baseball and love and living. A feeling of comfort surrounds and calms me and I feel an all-encompassing love for my fellow man, so strong that I must be experiencing what others who have found religious faith have experienced. I love all mankind. I love the fat lady.

Mr Revere reopens his zippered case and takes out the questionnaire. He studies it closely. I recognize that it is subtly different but I cannot say how. Perhaps only my perceptions are different.

Mr Revere smiles again, a smile of infinite sadness, and patience and love. "I'm sorry," he says. "You're not the one."

"But I've decided," I say.

"I'm aware of that. I appreciate . . . we appreciate that you want to help. I'm afraid I may have spoiled a very good ballgame for you . . ."

"But I want to . . ." my voice rises like a whining child's.

"I'm sorry." Mr Revere is extending his hand to me.

"I'm not good enough," I flare. People are staring at me.

The ballpark is very quiet. Houston is batting in the ninth, going out with a whimper. "I warn you, I'm a writer. I intend to write about this."

"Suit yourself," says Mr Revere calmly. "In fact, feel free. If we find the right party in the next few days, everything that transpired tonight will be obliterated from every memory. But if we don't . . ." he smiles again. "Why, who would believe you? If someone actually tracked me down, I'd plead innocence or senility or both. I'm just a retired gentleman from Iowa who came to Los Angeles for a few baseball games and sat beside a strange and rather disturbed young man. You'd end up looking rather foolish, I suspect. Anyway, no one should believe a silly old man who goes around baseball stadiums talking about resurrecting the dead," and he chuckles.

The game ends. Mr Revere makes his way briskly to the aisle and disappears in the crowd. I eventually edge my way to the aisle and down the steps for ten or fifteen rows. The Buffalo Brigade are now behind me. I turn to look at them. I scrunch myself against the railing and wait for them to catch up with me. There is something I have to know.

The fat lady huffs down the stairs towards me. I turn and face her in all her grossness. Her forehead and cheeks are blotched and somewhat out of focus, as though her face is covered by an inch or two of water.

"It was you I was going to do it for," I say. The fat lady stops in mid-waddle, puffs her cheeks like a child, and belches. "It was you that Manny Mota made the hit for. If you'd only realize it. Why don't you realize it?" I stand in the middle of the aisle facing up towards her. She is close enough for her sweetish odours of beer and perspiration to envelop me.

"Are you all right, fella?" a man behind her directs the words my way.

"Move along," somebody else shouts.

"Thurman Munson died for you," I say to the fat lady, who, three steps above me, glares down in bloodshot indignation.

"Oh, Jesus," says a voice behind her, a voice that is somewhere between an oath and a prayer.

Driving Toward the Moon

Driving Toward the Moon

I give the batter my best fastball on the outside corner. He takes it for a strike. There are runners on every base, dancing back and forth like those little snake-like noise makers people blow on New Year's Eve. I came in with the bases full and no one out. Got the first batter on a change-up, my best pitch, popped him up behind second. It's the top of the eighth and we're one run up. The next pitch is a slider, comes right in on his hands and he fouls it off. Dominuguez, the catcher, speaks no English except for "scrambled eggs" and "fuck off," but he knows how to handle a pitcher. I stare in at him and nod my head; he has two fingers down for the change-up. The tricky part is the arm motion. Warren Spahn said, "All there is to pitching is keeping the hitters off-stride." I have to use exactly the same motion as I do for the fastball, but, as the announcers always say, "take something off it." I decide it won't be a total change-up; I'll let up, but only five miles per hour or so. The batter stands tight as a spring, stiff as if his feet were embedded in concrete. I'm betting he'll think I'm going to waste one outside, try to make him go for a bad pitch. The ball is at his knees on the outside corner. He was guessing fastball and is finished his swing before the ball crosses the plate. The five hundred or so fans cheer. Two out, the worst of the pressure is off. Looks like another save coming up. I have six already and the season is barely a month old. I'm 4-1 with a 1.87 ERA.

This is Class D, or would be if there were still Class D leagues. Rookie League, they call it now. Wildly scattered teams in dismal, northern towns and cities: the Calgary Expos, Helena Phillies, Butte Copper Kings, Medicine Hat Blue Jays. Places so far from the real world a lot of us can't believe they exist. Small baseball parks perched like buttons on the prairies of Alberta, Montana, and Idaho. Ice-sports are what people are interested in out here: hockey, skiing, something odd called curling. Though the weather gets hot during the day, by nine or ten at night what fans are left need sweaters to keep warm, for a chill wind drifts down off the mountains even in high July. There is forever a threat of rain; in the evenings, as the watery floodlights crackle, the western sky darkens and lightning knifes across the clouds.

These are major-league farm teams, so there are no local players. We come here from high schools, junior colleges, try-out camps, foreign countries. The league operates from June to the end of August. A game a day. Winding highways, the smells of diesel exhaust, bad restaurants, and cramped seats. There's no place lonelier than the minor minor leagues.

"The tall one's got the hots for you," Bixby, the bullpen catcher, said to me while I was warming up, and without being obvious he angled his head toward two women who were sitting virtually alone about five rows up from where we were warming up in the right-field corner. I'd noticed them too, a compact blonde and a rangy girl with bronze-coloured hair. "You're lucky. I wish she'd look at me like that," Bixby went on. "I wish there were ten more like her. That's the big trouble with these bush league towns — too goddamn many little leaguers in the park and not enough beaver. Look at the stands! They must truck the little bastards down here after their games end."

I looked around. Bixby was right, the stands were studded with boy children, most in the bird-bright uniforms of Oakland, Houston, or San Francisco.

"Jesus but I wish I went for 'killer chicken' like Lopatio over there. It's a curse to like broads in a minor league town. Ain't that right, Lopatio?" The Dominican pitcher grinned wildly when he heard his name. I can only imagine how lonely he is, being so far from home and not speaking English. "You like little boys in baseball uniforms, si Lopatio?" The pitcher grinned and nodded, happy to have any attention paid to him. The rest of the bullpen roared.

"It's all in the tone of voice. If I'd sounded gruff he wouldn't have laughed. Like talking to a fuckin' dog. Dogs are so stupid you can call them every filthy name in the book as long as you use the right tone of voice. Now cats, they're different, they can sense who likes them. Speaking of which, if you don't claim that reddy-haired beauty up there, I'm gonna jump her bones in the parking lot."

"Trust me," I said, winking. "I wouldn't want to feel responsible for you doing something you don't really want to do."

On the road we stay in cheap, old, frame hotels that look out onto gravel alleys. They have sagging linoleum and frayed carpets, each room seedy and stifling, the john at the end of the hall. Our team, the Calgary Expos, ran ads in the newspapers asking for people willing to provide room and board for the players, close to the stadium. Those who responded virtually fought over the black players. There are very few black people this far north so they are a novelty. There was a line-up to take the two West Indian players: glistening black skin, white cat-like eyes, legs thin as thoroughbreds. The Nicaraguan and Venezuelan players are also very popular.

The people I was awarded to, a middle-aged government clerk and his wife, also a middle-aged government clerk, are chunky, pale people who might be dressmaker's dummies stuffed with porridge. My room is spotless, has no human odours, no indication it has ever been lived in. The hardwood has been waxed religiously. All the rooms are stuffed with elderly, unused furniture. On the dark end-table in the hall is a bland-coloured crocheted doily, its shape recognizable as the face of Jesus. A small shelf in the living room holds religious and inspirational pamphlets and books about Lawrence Welk and his pious entourage. There is a garish, ten-foot *Last Supper* above a fireplace that burns an electric log. Tom and Dora have a twenty-year-old son who has Down's Syndrome and is in a local institution where they visit him each Sunday after church. Dora serves meat and potatoes every supper, bacon and eggs every lunch. She often leaves an apple or cookies and milk on the kitchen table for me after a game. She also leaves religious tracts on the arm of the old chair where I sit to watch TV. In the middle of a meal she will sometimes sigh and say, "The Lord works in mysterious ways."

"Baseball is a clean game," Tom says vaguely. He never comes to the park to see us play.

Between pitches I look up at the two women Bixby was talking about. They have moved in closer since I came to the mound. The one whose eyes seem glued to me has bronze hair of medium length, the final inch or so curled slightly. She is smoking and as she talks with her friend gestures with her cigarette. Gold-rimmed glasses give her face a trimmed, business-like appearance; she is wearing faded jeans tucked into scuffed cowboy boots, and a red-and-white checkered blouse that reminds me of a tablecloth in an Italian restaurant. She holds a folded denim jacket on her knees. Her companion is shorter, plump, with severely cut blonde hair, and wears glasses with pointed blue-plastic rims.

"Lotsa luck, man," Bixby said to me when I got the call to go in with the bases loaded and nobody out. He winked and nodded his head toward the stands, "Just pretend she's gonna give you a blow job for every out you get." He slapped my shoulder, and waved to the girls in the stands. "Don't worry about the ballgame, just keep your mind on the beaver and everything will work out fine," he added, and I trotted off toward the mound.

The guy who could be the last batter of the inning thumps the plate with his bat and glares out at me. He is built like a small tractor. I deliver a rising fastball that ends out of the strike zone and he doesn't go for it. Dominuguez signals curve and I let one rip; my chest tightens as it fails to break, hangs over the plate fat as a grapefruit for what seems like forever before he swats it. Lucky I laid off a little, because he is just in front of it, and though he puts it out of the park it is foul by four or five feet. I sigh as the umpire fires a new ball out to me. In the stands the bronze-haired girl still has one hand covering her mouth and nose in a gesture of anticipated disaster. She has large hands; long, solid fingers with full, wide nails. I like women with big hands.

I send a slider in on his fists; he swings but the ball hits the handle and a weak comebacker hops into my glove making a sound like a rubber band popping. I take my time throwing to first, making sure the first baseman is in place, and I throw carefully to avoid any chance of error.

I trot off the field to the cheers of the crowd, the PA system blaring "When Johnny Comes Marching Home Again" because my name is Johnny. The announcer is sure to let everyone know every inning that some music dealer, who is really a philanthropist at heart, has donated the organ. The little weasel who plays it ought to have his hands amputated; he has a personal song for nearly every player: "Johnny" for me, for Bixby he plays the theme from *The Incredible Hulk* because an actor by that name played the main part in the series. He plays "Old Black Joe" for our lumbering black centre-fielder Joe Downing, who continually threatens to wait in the empty ballpark after a game and kill him.

As I walk in I tip my cap to the crowd, making certain I look right at the two women.

I waste no time setting the Idaho Falls team down in the ninth. Save number seven; my ERA will be down a few points. After the usual congratulations from my team-mates, instead of heading off across the field for the trailer-clubhouse I stay near the dugout railing, where there are always a few kids wanting autographs. I see the girls moving step by step down the bleachers toward the exit behind home. The bronze-haired woman is carrying a program, and as they pass I stop writing and wave my pen in her direction. She smiles, and she and her friend wait as I sign programs and bits of paper for the little leaguers.

"Who's it for?" I ask when she finally thrusts the program toward me. A trick Bixby has taught me. "Great way to find out names," he said. "Once you get the name, you ask for the phone number. While they're ho-humming over that you invite them out for a drink. Three drinks and drop the laundry, works every time."

"You really did a great job," says the blonde. She is about twenty-five, with peachy skin and an upturned nose.

"Rose," says the tall one, leaving her hand on the program so that our fingers rub together ever so slightly. And from that one word I can tell she is American, like me. California would be my first guess but maybe Texas, possibly Oklahoma.

I write "For Rose," I want to put "with love," or "in anticipation," or "I want you," but instead I write the standard "with best wishes."

"Where are you from?" I say. "You sound Californian."

We are interrupted by Bixby. "All right, I'll sign too, if you really want me to," he says pushing in beside me. "You understand I don't usually give autographs . . ." He grabs the program from my left hand and the pen from my right. "Now, what did you say your name was?" he says to the blonde.

"Bonnie," she replies, laughing.

"Bonnie," he repeats, staring straight into her eyes, and I know he is deciding how raunchy he can be with her without offending her. Sometimes, in fact often, Bixby goes too far too quickly. "I used to have a dog named Bonnie," he says. "A little brown-eyed cocker spaniel used to sleep with me every night," and he stares into her face with his wide, innocent, blue eyes. Bixby is about six-foot-four and has lemon-coloured hair that falls over his eyes even when he is wearing his baseball cap. "Let's see," he says, waving the pen. "For Bonnie, who reminds me of someone I used to sleep with," he says as he writes. Rose and Bonnie both laugh. "By the way, where are we going?" he says, handing the program to Bonnie.

The girls look puzzled. "You mean Johnny hasn't asked you yet? Just like him. Meet us in the parking lot. Mine's the blue and white Camaro with Georgia plates right behind the club-house. Just pull your car up beside it and wait. We'll be out in-side of fifteen minutes." And he grabs me by the arm and turns me around where I can see the last of the players disappearing through the centrefield gate.

"I'm married," I hear Bonnie say.

"Orange County," says Rose. "How did you know?"

"Do you suppose they'll be there?" I say to Bixby in the clubhouse.

"Yours is in heat, man. They'll be there. My Bonnie won't abandon her friend."

Rose: I want to feel her fingers all over my body. She has hazel eyes that appear flat and liquid behind her glasses. She is at least five-ten. Oh, how I like the tall ones.

I am through my shower and dressed in less than five minutes.

"Make 'em wait," says Bixby when I reach in and turn off his shower. "Never let a broad know you're anxious, Johnny. If they're not there we'll go find two more. The way you treat women you'll end up married in no time. Broads are just dying to latch onto polite young men who are always on time. They have a handbook, you know. Behind 'polite, respectful, and on time,' there's an asterisk, and when they look to the bottom of the page it reads 'Marry this one before he gets away.' Treat 'em rough, Johnny, tell 'em nothing, and always leave 'em crying."

"Yeah, I know, women are like shotguns, should be kept loaded and standing in a corner."

Bixby laughs heartily as he towels his hair. "That's my man. Only you got to say it like you believe it, Johnny."

When we reach the parking lot the girls are sitting in a maroon and white Buick with mustard-yellow Alberta licence plates. The usual hassle about cars develops. The Buick belongs to Rose. Should we take two cars? Who rides where? I don't even mention that the sleazy, scum-green Plymouth on the other side of Bixby's car is mine. It used to be a taxi; I bought it in South Carolina, right after the Orioles sold me to the Expos and they assigned me up here. The other Rookie

Leagues are in Florida and California, but I get signed by a team whose farm club is just off the edge of the earth.

We settle on Bixby's car, but the girls ride in the back. Bonnie's idea. Bonnie is nervous and ill at ease. She tells us about five times that she is married, adding "happily" the last two or three. Bix and I joke about our manager, whom we call Skip. A guy who has the personality of a geek and the same IQ as the batting cage. I keep watching Rose over the back of the seat. Her face is oval, her chin round with a dimple that looks like a baby has poked it with an exploring finger. Her lips are prominent and sensual. Our eyes keep meeting and my inclination is to leap over the seat and take her in my arms.

At the bar, a quiet place dark enough to be a cellar, stuffed with circular booths upholstered in cool, dark-red leather, we make nervous conversation. I sit next to Rose, and a moment later without her seeming to move, her thigh is solidly pressed against mine.

To keep the conversation going I tell the story of my rather odd landlords: " 'We would frown on you bringing a person of the opposite sex into your room,' " I say, imitating Tom's high whisper. " 'However, you may feel free to have friends in the living room on the condition that no alcoholic beverages will be served.' I just smiled obligingly and nodded. 'Yassuh, Massa Tom,' I was tempted to say. No wonder these home-sharers wanted black players. I wonder how the ones who got one are getting along with them? I can imagine Tom and Dora telling one of those West Indian kids in tight slacks and patent-leather shoes that he can't have guests in his room while he's discoing around the kitchen."

We all laughed comfortably.

"You know what I was afraid of while I was waiting in the parking lot?" Rose whispers to me. "That I wouldn't recognize you without your baseball uniform." She laughs. Her bottom teeth are climbing over each other. I don't know when I have ever wanted a woman more. I realize we are both exhibiting a great deal of self-restraint.

Beside us Bix is sort of chasing Bonnie around the circular booth. He moves close to her, puts an arm around her shoulder; she slides away moving along the smooth leather until she is next to Rose. Then she reaches back and drags her drink after her. "This is silly," she says, then sort of straight-arms Bix, the flat of her hand against his chest, until he grins and moves back around the table.

Rose lights a cigarette. Her tongue wets her lips as she exhales. I let my right hand drop from the table as casually as I can and rest my fingers on her denim thigh. She shudders and presses harder against me.

Bix loves to tell stories, especially if they top mine. We order a second round of drinks, over Bonnie's protests, while Bix tells the story of *his* landlady. "I was at my place of detention for one day before we opened the season with a week on the road," Bix begins. "Fat, middle-aged high-school teacher, wears fluorescent mumus and has blue-black sausage curls, little draw-string mouth like a 1920s movie star. The whole house smells of floor-wax and mothballs. You know how many moths you have to kill to get those things?"

The girls laugh politely. I reach across and put my hand on top of Rose's hand, where it rests beside her glass. The thrill of her races up my arm like electric current.

"House is stuffed full of kitsch: velvet paintings of bull-fighters and teary-eyed children, ornaments made from cut-up gallon tins, the edges curled up like flowers and spray-painted gold and silver, lampshades still covered in plastic. Like everybody's grandmothers'. The wallpaper in the dining room was about 10,000 pictures of Jesus' head with a green halo around it. A Bible on every end-table and two in my room. And she had this dog, one of those yappy little mothers about three inches tall, a wiggling dustmop of a dog. While she's showing me my room he yaps around my legs and chews on my shoelaces. 'Oh, Jose loves you,' says the teacher. 'I never rent to anyone unless Jose loves them. I've had him for nine years.' I'd like to tell her, 'Lady, your dog doesn't know love from crankcase oil.' I was telling Johnny earlier about how dumb dogs are. I'd like to punt the little fucker into next week, but does he know that?"

Rose slowly turns her hand over and twines her fingers with

mine. Then, taking a deep drag on her cigarette, she looks uneasily at Bonnie.

"A real man-hater, that landlady," Bix goes on. " 'I bet you've abandoned a poor wife and family somewhere to come up here with this . . . baseball team.' She pronounced *baseball team* like syphilis. 'I'm divorced,' I tell her, and she nods knowingly. 'No women in your room,' she tells me in no uncertain terms. And when I look at her like she's crazy . . . 'They have motels for that sort of thing,' she says. 'I won't tolerate anything immoral in my home.'

"How long before the twentieth century is gonna reach this part of the country, I think. But I don't say anything. What the hell, I'll buy a pair of panties and stash them under the bed. I'll leave condoms around the room for her to find. When I've got her watching me close I slip a bra in with my washing. She'll be crazy spying on me before the season ends.

"But what I didn't know is how crazy she really is. Like I said, I was only there one day and then gone for nine. Everything was cool when I came back. I noticed the dog wasn't around, so just to be polite I asked about him at supper. Teacher is not looking well, wearing a black silk mumu and about a pound of lipstick, eyeshadow, and rouge. Enough to make a toilet vomit. Well, she gets all teary and tells me Jose dropped dead the day after I left. Heart attack, her vet says, but I bet the dog just realized how ugly she was and handed over his yappy little soul.

"After supper I see the grave as I go out the back door. The earth is all fresh-dug on top, and there is a bouquet of plastic flowers and the whole grave is surrounded by a white plastic fence. Weird. Later, while I'm watching TV, she sits across the room, tears dripping down her face. She's wearing as much make-up as a Japanese actor and the colours are all running together as she cries.

" 'Why don't you get yourself another dog?' I say. 'It might help you to feel better.' I mean she looks pathetic, sitting there snuffling, all in black, big as a hippo. I suppose she really liked the dog; she's already told me about five times how her husband had left her for another woman. She couldn't understand it. 'I was a good cook,' she said.

" 'Oh, no,' she says in reply to my question. 'I could never get a dog to take Jose's place. He'll be waiting for me on the other side. Jose was Pentecostal, you know.' "

" 'Oh, really?' was all I could muster."

" 'Oh yes, he was very devout,' she says. 'He'll be waiting for me.' She's put away a fifth of vodka since supper. I didn't think Pentecostals were supposed to drink anything stronger than their bath water.''

Bonnie insists that we leave because her husband will be worrying. Outside, Bix does manage to pull her into the front seat with him, but she steadfastly refuses to sit anywhere near him. I take both of Rose's hands in mine and lean over to kiss her, but as I do she moves away slightly, forcing my face into the crook of her neck. She is wearing a satiny top that feels cool against my skin.

"Not yet," she whispers. As she leans down her lips touch my ear. I don't understand the feelings that pass through me like bullets. There is so much more than pure sexual desire. As we move along we are unable to concentrate on whatever story Bix is telling. We are like magnet and metal, longing. I am struck by the absurd thought that until now I thought it was a thrill to strike out the side.

Rose leans forward and interrupts Bix. "Bonnie only lives a few blocks from here, you can drop her off on the way to the ballpark. I'll drop Johnny off . . ." Bix practically does a wheelie with the Camaro. I can only imagine what he had planned for Bonnie in the quiet of the parking lot. As Bonnie begins directing Bix toward her home, she shoots Rose a relieved yet suspicious glance. Rose has moved across to the passenger window and is smoking prettily.

Bix, never one to stay annoyed for long, launches into a raunchy song about freckles on various parts of his body. After much hassling he extracts Bonnie's phone number at work, and we roar off toward the ballpark.

"Be cool, guys," Bix says as we exit. We both smile and wave as the car sprays gravel and dust.

"I'm sorry Bonnie was so . . ."

"Married," I say, as Rose unlocks her car.

As soon as we are seated in her car in the silent parking lot I reach over and touch Rose's arm. In response she flings herself into my arms, our mouths colliding. We settle into a wild tongue-touching kiss. When our lips part I kiss across her cheek and down her neck.

"I thought I was going to be able to keep myself from doing that," she whispers. "I was going to shake hands with you at your door." She laughs nervously. Our lips brush again, and we settle into another long, sweet kiss, her cool-fingered hand is inside my shirt.

When we come up for air I say, "I've told you about where I live. How about you? Do you have a place where we can go?" Her glasses are already smudged. Her lips, bearing no cosmetics, seem to be swollen slightly by her passion. Before she answers she kisses me again, her tongue wild in my mouth. "I'm married too," she whispers, kissing me again in a way that tells me it doesn't matter at all.

The next morning the team went on the road for eight days. No way to call her. No place to write. She works for an oil company but I don't remember which one. I think she told me her last name but I either didn't catch it or don't remember.

The first night on the road, in Helena, I come in in the seventh, again with the bases loaded, but this time Bixby is catching. "Pretend my glove is her old man's face. The only thing between the ball and his face is some turkey's bat." "I don't know anything about her husband," I almost say, realizing at the last instant how foolish it would sound. Bix is only trying to psyche me up. There is the thought of someone else touching her. Of her liking it. "Put some smoke on it, man," says Bix.

The first two batters never see the ball. The third trickles down to first base. We score in the eighth. Another win. My ERA is down to 1.74.

The next night, while we are warming up, a civilian comes toward the bullpen holding an envelope. "One of you guys Johnnie Scott?" he says.

"I am."

I've never seen her handwriting before. It is oversized and round. The card is addressed to me in care of the Calgary Expos at the Helena Stadium. It is one of those write-your-own-message cards, a picture of a boy and girl, arms about each other's waists, walking into a pastoral scene. Inside, in the same round script, are the words "I love you." No signature. When no one is looking I take the card into the dressing room, stash it at the bottom of my bag, then, since the room is empty, I take it out, study it, smiling like an idiot. I look guiltily around, press my lips against the words "I love you," and replace the card.

I've always thought I cared more about baseball than anything in the world. I've shared Bixby's views, if not about women, about baseball. I'm comfortable being a relief pitcher and I wouldn't change it for any other position. Whenever I come in I can always see the end in sight. If I play it right I never have to face the same batter twice. Six outs, five, four, maybe only a couple, that's all I have to look for. I can put my whole physical and mental self into every pitch. "What does it matter?" I hear myself asking. "What does it matter if Rose isn't there to watch me, if she isn't waiting after a game, or when I get home from a road trip?" I have never dreamed anything could take on the importance of baseball in my life. The very idea of it confuses me. "Later," I have always said. "Later, when I'm established, I will think about love."

"Keep your head screwed on straight," Bix tells me. "No bubbles in your blood. Don't go thinking with your dork. Baseball first, beaver second, always. Half the world is made up of beaver, Johnny. If you miss out on one there's a hundred to take her place." I can't argue with him. I can only act on how I feel, and right now I'm in love with Rose.

She and Bonnie are in the same seats near the bullpen at our next home game. After I wave to them they move down to the first row; a quarrelsome wind gusts and there is a definite threat of rain. Rose wears her denim jacket. We are ahead by eight runs so I don't even have to warm up. I spend most of the evening leaning on the railing to the stands, joking about Bixby who is catching the game. My behaviour puzzles me; it is as though I am in junior high again. I show off by tossing and spinning a ball every way I know, and all I do is melt when Rose smiles and laughs to show she appreciates what I'm doing. I feel very awkward; I don't know what is expected of me.

It is the eighth inning before I finally say, "Are we going for a drink after?"

"I can't," Bonnie says quickly.

"We came in Bonnie's car tonight," says Rose.

"No problem, I can drop you off," I say. I give Rose my car keys so she can wait there for me. It is all so awkward and transparent.

We don't even drive around or go for a drink. We just sit in my old Plymouth with the terry-cloth seat covers, me sipping a can of Diet Pepsi, Rose smoking, our hands touching lightly, until the last of the fans and players are gone, and my car sits alone in the dark parking lot. I have only dreamed of desiring a woman the way I want Rose: of two people being all over each other the way we are. "You know I had that feeling again while I was waiting that I wouldn't know you without your uniform on," Rose whispers.

"Still feeling that way?"

"I'd know you anywhere, in uniform or naked. I'm still not sure about street clothes." The only thing either of us are wearing are Rose's smudged glasses. "I like to look at you while we make love, and without these everything is a blur." The windows of the car are fogged, the interior heavy with the odours of our love-making. The windows have to remain closed because of the dragonfly-sized mosquitoes.

Eventually we go to an all-night café, hold hands under the table and talk. I tell Rose my life story, from being born near Chapel Hill, to my one year at North Carolina University, how I was cut from the baseball squad, dropped out, spent two years working nights in a fast-food joint and days pitching to a target nailed to a garage wall. I tell her about my brother who has more talent for baseball than I'll ever have but wastes it driving stock cars and drinking beer, and about my father, the Ugly American, who is VP of a cotton mill. I tell her of the no-hitter I pitched in high school, and for probably far too long about a girl I lived with for a year, named June-Star Whelan, who had blue eyes you could drown in and chewed gum while we made love.

It is only when I am alone in my stuffy, antiseptic room, or in a creaking hotel bed on the road, that I realize Rose has told me almost nothing about herself. She seems to carry no ID. She has a money clip, like a man, in the back pocket of her jeans.

"I moved to Calgary from California when I was sixteen." I have to assume the rest. She must have come with her family. Her father is probably in oil; Calgary is full of American oil people. "I got married when I was eighteen. My child was born the next year." I don't know the name of the husband, or the child, or the sex of the child. Rose turns aside my questions with kisses. "It's not important," she says over and over.

It is very late when I drop her off down the block from where she lives in a large, ranch-style home, high on a ridge on the western edge of the city.

The next evening Rose is alone in the stands near the bullpen.

"Where's your friend?"

"She won't come with me anymore." She pauses. "She's got eyes."

"Not much of a friend."

"She wants what's best for me."

In my car, deep in the night, she finally talks a little of herself. "I've got a little girl, sort of. We live with his mother. We're saving to buy our own house. She babysits so I can work full time. She's never let me do anything on my own. The first word the baby said was 'Gramma.'"

I tried to imagine in what light Rose sees me. "You're like the coloured birds I used to see darting through the trees when I was a kid," she said to me last night. "Wherever there's summer there's baseball, Canada, the States, Mexico, Japan, all those little countries in Central America. I read once that they stop their wars for baseball games. They give the good left-handed guerrilla pitcher safe passage in from the hills. He pitches the game, goes back into hiding; the next day some of his team-mates try to hunt him down and kill him.''

I try to imagine a man I don't know alone in a bedroom full of Rose's delicious odours. "Your husband? What do you tell him?''

"He sleeps soundly.''

"What about us? We can find a place together. Will you come back to Carolina with me when the season ends?''

"Maybe when the season ends. But I can't leave now. He'd kill me if I told him I was leaving. He said that once. 'I'd kill you if you left me,' he said. He doesn't talk much. When he says something he means it.''

"You're not going to do anything foolish, are you?'' Bixby says to me a day or two later. "Listen, I'm your friend. Trust me, she's only a broad. You haven't got to the 'I love you' stage yet, have you?'' He looks me square in the eyes and I feel like I'm impaled by his gaze. I can't look anybody in the eye and lie to them.

"Sort of,'' I say.

"Johnny, the world's paved with beaver. Use all you want but don't get attached to it.''

"I feel differently about Rose,'' I say lamely.

"Hey, she's a beautiful girl. I'm sure she's nice. Have fun until the season's over. Then make a new start. We're gonna play in the Mexican leagues, right. Don't tie yourself down.''

"Right,'' I say reluctantly.

"I'll think about marriage after I retire from the Bigs,'' says Bixby. "We'll never get there if we tie ourselves down, right?''

I don't answer him and I can tell he's worried.

"Maybe you should talk to Skip about it?'' he says tentatively.

"Come on, Bix,'' I shout.

"Yeah, right. Fifty years old and never been past Triple A. Dribbles Redman down the front of his uniform. Must have something on somebody high up in the organization, but nothing serious or he'd be a first base coach in the Bigs; that's where they put the brain-damaged, and guys who teach their players to chase runners down to the wrong base. Yeah, he's a nobody. But he's been dragging a wife around with him for thirty years; he might be able to give you some valuable advice.''

The next afternoon it rained. Looked like the mountains were rumbling down to crush us, the clouds were deep and black-wild. There would be no baseball game. No way to see Rose. I drove up the ridge past her house, then back down the hill to a shopping centre with a huge bar called Castle Mountain.

I spotted the Buick in the parking lot and my heart began to beat faster. Then I realized Rose didn't take the car to work. I parked next to it. There was a black lunch box resting on the red-leather upholstery. Of course, he worked outdoors, he would have been rained out too. Eventually a group of young men emerged and moved jerkily across the rainy parking lot. Suddenly I knew which one he was: a compact man with a white tee-shirt stretched over the beginning of a beer belly, his hair long and sun-bleached where it showed beneath a yellow hard-hat. He wore cement-stained blue-jeans and heavy construction boots. His weather-reddened face was wide and jovial. He splashed through the puddles and got into the car next to me, took a cigarette from a pack in his shirt pocket and ducked his head as he used the car lighter.

I wonder if what Rose said of him is true? Will he kill her if she leaves him? Does he think his wife has been going to baseball games with her girlfriend and out for a drink afterward? Does he care? Has she done this before? No. I know better. ''When I saw you,'' Rose said, ''I felt like electricity was being shot through me. I know that's trite. I've never acted this way before. Never dreamed I would. Bonnie can't believe I'm doing what I'm doing, and neither can I. But I'm not going to stop,'' she added, turning her face to me to be kissed.

An angry husband. A child.

''I'd kill you if you left me.'' I conjure up newspaper headlines: *Baseball Player Slain in Love Triangle*. My biggest worry used to be if my curve was breaking down-and-in or not. ''He's going fishing with his friends, late Friday to late Sunday,'' Rose says before the next game. ''I've already told them

Bonnie and I are going to Edmonton to visit her sister. We'll have the whole weekend to ourselves." The night is heavily overcast, and Rose is one of about two dozen fans in the park.

"Do you want to go somewhere? I've never been to the mountains, we could . . ."

"Too many people to see us," says Rose. We settle on renting a motel room. There are a row of motels across from the baseball and football stadiums. "They even have restaurants, if we ever want food," says Rose, and forgetting where she is she reaches over the railing to touch my arm.

Dominuguez is catching, so Bixby is with me in the bullpen. When I'm called on to loosen up, Bixby pleads a cramp and gets one of the other catchers to warm me up. I don't concentrate very well as I watch out of the corner of my eye while Bixby talks furiously with Rose.

"He's dangerous," Rose says later. "Appealed to all my 'good instincts.' I'm supposed to feel guilty if your career suffers because of me."

I'm called in in the ninth, face three batters: two doubles and a single. I'm replaced. Back in the bullpen Bixby doesn't say anything, but his smile says "I told you so."

In what she claims is her final gesture of friendship, Bonnie picks Rose up on Friday evening and delivers her to a restaurant next to the motel I have reserved. "If she doesn't know where we're staying then she can't cause either of us any trouble," Rose says to me.

"You don't trust her," I say.

"It's just safer," says Rose.

For the first time we make love in a bed, slowly and with infinite pleasure. I imagine we are like pictures I've seen of creatures growing in warm liquid.

Saturday night and Sunday afternoon there are baseball games. I am distracted, miss easy plays, walk batters; I take the loss Sunday. I don't care very much; I am more anxious to get back to Rose.

That evening we go for a drive. I cruise around the city for a while, stop and buy us each a cold soft drink.

"Which way now?" I ask.

"Just drive toward the moon," says Rose. She lays back languidly, her head tipped back, resting on the frame of the open passenger window. The moon hangs high and full in the southeast, pale in the evening sky looking as though it has thumb smudges on it.

Eventually I get on a thread-like secondary highway, the moon in front of us, brighter now, like pewter caught in the beam of a searchlight. The country is dark and silent. Occasionally an insect ticks against the windshield. Our headlights and the moon offer the only brightness.

"We're not going back, are we?" I finally say.

Rose snuggles close to me, her head on my shoulder, her hand on my thigh. I think of the tartness of her mouth, the spectacular warmth of her, how when we finally stop we'll cover each other with our mouths. My tongue on her fingers . . . .

Rose starts to speak. "If Bonnie doesn't, Bixby will . . ." she says.

"Don't say anything practical."

Rose moves her hand between my legs. "Mmm," she says.

"Tomorrow I'll call Skip. There are other Rookie Leagues. I'm good enough for them to care."

"Keep driving toward the moon," Rose whispers.

Barefoot and Pregnant
in Des Moines

Barefoot and Pregnant
in Des Moines

"We're not poor anymore," I say, almost shout. "We can afford for you to fly out and join me, any time you want to."

The French doors are closed and the air conditioner breathes unobtrusively in the background, like a large, sleeping pet. Gwen is wearing a dress the colour of green liqueur. Her nyloned legs are crossed delicately at the ankles; her short, dark hair gleams enticingly. She sits forward on the sofa, her green eyes intent. Her lipstick and nail polish are a matching cardinal red.

When Gwen is like this, intent, sincere, lips slightly parted, eyes focused on my face waiting for me to say something, I find it is almost impossible to believe she doesn't understand my feelings, doesn't comprehend how she tears me to pieces with her indifference, her deception. She is so darkly beautiful; my heart feels like a frog held in cupped hands.

"Look," I go on, digging a Mets schedule from the pocket of my team jacket. "There's at least a ten-day home stand almost every month. Once, here in July, we're home for eight days, on the road for three, then back in New York for nine days. We could have almost three weeks together. You don't have to come to the games, you know that. You can go to plays and concerts . . .''

"I can hardly drag Charlene to plays, concerts, and ball-games," Gwen says in her easy, languid New Orleans drawl. Her voice is so naturally pleasant, I have to listen closely for inflections in order to tell when she is cross or perturbed.

"You can hire a babysitter," I counter.

"Really, Millard, you know what those New York people are like . . . so . . . irresponsible. I couldn't leave Charlene with one of them. Besides, she gets so cranky when she's away from home."

Millard! Gwen only uses my given name when we're having a serious discussion. I've been known as Dude, ever since Little League. One of the trivia questions TV announcers ask during the seventh inning is, "What is Dude Atchison's given name?"

For almost three months, since about Christmas, I've been pushing Gwen to come right out and let me know how much time we're gonna have together this coming season. Since Christmas she's called me Millard more than she ever has.

Gwen's grand-daddy was an important man in New Orleans society around the turn of the century. He owned an undertaking parlour and lived in a fancy three-storey frame house on Prytania Street. Gwen's mama still has a photograph of that fancy house; along with a photograph of her daddy, a bald-headed man with a vegetable-brush moustache and round glasses, him standing by a table loaded with expensive china and linens. Gwen's family lost their money during the depression. Her grand-daddy died in the charity ward of a hospital. Her daddy ran off with a cocktail waitress, to California, about the time she was seven years old

Having money is what's caused all our trouble. Who'd ever think that? When I was in the minors, barely making enough to live on, Gwen didn't mind being with me. She didn't mind the seedy little studio apartment in Butte, Montana, when I played for the Butte Copper Kings in Rookie League, or that basement in Burlington, Iowa, where the black water bugs, big as quarters, clicked across the linoleum at daybreak. Part of the reason she didn't mind was we didn't have things any better here in New Orleans. The first off-season after we were married we lived in her mother's back bedroom. Her mama lived in this tiny frame house where the siding hadn't been painted for so long it had gone back to the colour of a moth, where the yard was overgrown, and close enough to downtown to be unsafe for any of us to go walking after dark.

In those days we were glad to get away to training camp, happy to be able to make love with abandon, not having to worry about the springs protesting too loudly, or Gwen's mother wrinkling up her nose when we came back into the tiny living room; Gwen able to cry out her passion, not having to bite the pillow or my shoulder in order to keep silent.

I'm really surprised that we're not any happier, living in this glass and brick wonder the way we do. I'm told it's worth a half-million dollars. The house sits on about five acres bordering Jefferson Parish; the lawn rolls down toward our own bayou, wide as a freeway, where drooping cypress wade in the tepid water. I have my own pitching machine, and no matter how far I hit the baseballs it flings at me, they land on my own property.

There are a lot of things in our life that aren't right. The first being Gwen and I had agreed not to have children. It must have been about our second date that the subject came up.

"I never want to have any kids," I said.

"All boys talk that way," Gwen replied, and smiled, rather condescingly.

"No, I'm serious," I said. I reached across and touched her hand; her fingers were cool and her whole hand so delicate it might have been made of lace. We were sitting in an ice cream shop, at a table with a clear glass top and white wrought-iron insect legs. "I decided long ago that I never want children. People shouldn't have children unless they truly want them. And I can't imagine ever wanting one."

"Oh, well, I guess it isn't something we have to worry about right away," Gwen said, and smiled that same smile. I would never be sure if it was enigma, admiration, or contempt.

Gwen was wearing a starched white top and a pleated skirt

the colour of lemons. Her hair was razor-cut and every hair
knew where it belonged. Her eyes were green with flecks of
gold and the freckles across the bridge of her nose left me
breathless.

The subject of children came up often over the winter as we
got more and more serious about each other.

"Where would you be if your parents hadn't wanted
children," Gwen's mother would say and laugh lightly. She is
a horse-faced woman with protruding teeth, young enough that
she and Gwen are more like girlfriends than mother and
daughter. She is good natured, but a woman who always gets
her way.

Looking back I think she had more input about this house
than I realized. She occupies a whole suite of rooms and has
her own rose garden and a private gardener. Where would I
be, indeed? Where would she be if I couldn't hit a baseball 400
feet. "Dude, you cover the outfield like a condom," the best
sportswriter in America said to me. "I'll think up some other
image to use in my damn family newspaper," he went on,
"but I just want you to know what I'd like to write about you."

Never trust anyone to change. I guess that's the lesson I'm
learning. It's a hard lesson. Your spots are painted on by
parents, sometimes branded on. They can't be scraped off,
worn off, or loved off.

"Mother says you'll change after we're married," Gwen
said to me once.

"I thought I'd made myself pretty clear," I said. "Like you
I didn't have a daddy around, but I had a mother who whined
to anyone who'd listen, about what a burden I was and how I'd
ruined her life. I reckon she's still in Oklahoma City, in a
yellow stucco apartment that don't even have air conditioning.
Still whining. Well I might be just as bad a parent as she is. I'm
never gonna have children; if you have any trouble accepting
that, break the engagement."

There is a special organization for couples who have opted
not to have children. They even have a newsletter, *Optional
Parenthood Today*. I joined, and made sure Gwen read the
newsletter. I was more fair than anyone could have asked.

I tried to explain to Gwen what I saw on the road. The agony players went through being part-time fathers, scarcely knowing their children, being treated like strangers, like intruders in their own homes during the off-season. Those same men were always delighted to hit the road; they showed up days early for spring training, glad to get away from the strangers who were their family.

Worse still were the ones who really cared and still lost. Buck Wallin, our starting catcher last year, was a veteran of four years in the majors and five in the minors. He was only 27, but he'd married his high school sweetheart and she'd stayed at home in Poston, Alabama, had three kids and a house the size of a country club. Buck flew her and the kids up for a week or so a couple of times a season and he'd fly home over all-star break and any other chance he got. But she left him. Moved in with the owner of the feed mill, a man Buck's age who'd inherited the business from his daddy. In mid-September she sent Buck a letter saying not to come home when the season ended, said she'd been "going with" her special friend for two years, that the kids were beginning to call him daddy and that it would be best if he didn't disrupt their lives anymore.

The lives of a lot of the other players might have been less trying emotionally but equally savage in their own way. Men of 30 or less, divorced, remarried, two, three, four times. Children scattered like pennies across America. Men ravaged financially, making hundreds of thousands a year but saddled by enormous debts: alimony, child support; their houses long occupied by strangers, though the player paid the mortgage. The ends of their careers looming cold as icebergs on the horizon.

"I've got nothing to show for 14 seasons but a tired right arm, three rich ex-wives, and a drinking problem," one veteran pitcher told me, sitting naked in a clammy-floored locker room, staring into his Budweiser as if it were infinity.

Baseball players have never been good risks to stay married. I've always known that and I've always been determined to be different. It doesn't matter how much you love a woman or how much she loves you, if you're away from each other for months at a time, the relationship dies.

"I want my wife with me *all* the time," I say to Gwen. "You agreed to that. You wanted that."

"Things are different now; we have another person to consider . . ."

I've taken a lot of guff from the other players about Gwen travelling with me full time, but it's been good-natured and most of it has been envy.

I've never been unfaithful to Gwen. Other guys can do what they wish with the pretty, butterfly-like girls who flutter around the hotels and the players' gate, waiting to be collected.

"Hell, boy, why you want to drag a wife along?" one of the veterans asked me. He said *wife* as if he were describing a car that wouldn't start. "I got an old lady, but I keep her barefoot and pregnant in Des Moines. I see her over all-star break and during the off-season. As it should be. What more could anybody want? She's a good woman. I don't interfere with her life. She don't interfere with mine. When I get released, I ain't never gonna retire as long as I can lift a bat with two hands. Know what I'm gonna miss most? Them ladies in the hotel lobbies, or sittin' up on a bar stool, cool as salad, with a smile and a hug, all painted up pretty and waitin' to be tasted. I don't know how I'll get along without them."

I've always made it clear to everyone, including Gwen, that I didn't want to be involved in those kind of situations. Gwen saw how the other players acted; I can't understand why she wants to cast me out there into a world full of girls bright as tropical birds, most of them uniform freaks, groupies, looking for excitement, danger, wearing their sexuality like a team pennant. All I want is my wife with me. I don't want to go home to a stranger at the end of a season or the end of a career.

At first I was even dumb enough to believe that old-timer when he told me his family was in Des Moines. I found out later that was just an expression to cover the way wives and families were regarded in general. "Where's your old lady?" "Barefoot and pregnant in Des Moines."

Gwen's never been barefoot poor. Will never have to be. But two years ago, after I hit 38 home runs in my rookie year with the Mets, after management tore up my contract, without even asking me, and rewrote me a dandy that means I'll never have to sell insurance, used cars, or beg some sport freak to get me a beer distributorship after I retire, Gwen went and got herself pregnant.

She never asked or begged or argued, or said, "Go to hell, I'm going to have a baby whether you want one or not." Just quit taking the pill without ever discussing it with me. Was three months along before she told me. It was about two years ago now, me getting ready for spring training; the foundations for this house were already in and we were discussing room sizes and open-beam ceilings with the architect. It was right in the middle of making love that she told me. I read in one of them women's magazines Gwen and her mother keep around that you're supposed to break bad news to someone when they're doing something they like, like eating a steak dinner or something. Gwen must have read that article too.

"Honey," she said, and she pulled me close to stop my body moving against her. "We probably should think about takin' it a little easy. We got a baby growin' inside there now." Never an apology for deceiving me. Calm as if she just bought a new plant for the living room.

Of course Gwen couldn't travel out to see me in New York and on the road but a few times that season. The baby was born the first of September. Last season she couldn't take a new baby on the road at all. Charlene's about a year-and-a-half old now. Plenty old enough to travel.

But Gwen sits cool as a dewy bush first thing in the morning. She don't listen to me. Just brushes aside everything I say, the way she's been brushing me aside ever since she got pregnant. I can't believe anyone can change so much. We used to have some fine times in bed. But not anymore. Seems like Gwen don't think it's right for rich ladies to enjoy themselves in bed. I don't know how I could have been so fooled. "Shh, now, or mama will hear us,'' she'll say. She never said that when we had the back bedroom in that little old house downtown, and then her mama was only two sheets of wallpaper away. "If we carry on so, we'll wake the baby,'' is something else she says. I got no argument for that. Even in this house that's big as the whole neighbourhood I was raised in, Gwen's got the nursery right next to our room. There is even a connecting door.

I got no argument for anything that's happening to me. I just turn away, open the French doors and feel the solid wall of humid air hit me as I walk across the white tiles of the patio and down the rolling lawn to where I keep my pitching machine.

I think my books are just about all full of green stamps.

About twice a year my papa stopped by Oklahoma City to visit me. He tried to explain to me once, when I was about 14, how come he and mother had separated.

"I just collected the hurt and the wrongs and the frustration; I filed them away like a person pastes green stamps in a booklet,'' was part of what he said to me. "You know what those are, son; when you get so many booklets full, why you cash them in on a prize.

"One day, it was just like somebody sent me a letter or called me up long distance; I just knew that all the books of green stamps were full, and when I looked at your mama I just didn't care anymore. She'd drained me, whittled me down over the years until I didn't love her anymore. After that, except for you, leaving was easy.''

Now I know how my father must have felt as he weighed and measured the pros and cons. Charlene, my daughter, is like holding an armful of cherry blossoms. Like me, one corner of her mouth pulls down when she smiles. When I look at her my heart aches with love. Then I look at Gwen and I can't forgive her treachery.

"Gwen, I want you to come with me to training camp.'' I am pacing back and forth on the deep white carpet. "We don't have to skimp anymore. I'll get us the best room at the best hotel.'' I rush on before she has a chance to say anything. "We can hire a full-time babysitter for Charlene. We'll have lots of free time for ourselves. We can even rent a house if you want to. Would you like that?''

I stop and look closely at Gwen, waiting for her beautiful features to form into a smile, the way they used to when I told her I'd gone four-for-five and hit two homers. The way they did when I traded the coughing old Plymouth for a Lincoln, the way they did when I scrounged tickets to the Willie Nelson concert in New York, the way they did when we got invited backstage 'cause Willie wanted to meet me.

She is silent for a long time. Her silences defeat me. I look at her in her dress the cool colour of a mint drink. She has the false prettiness of a mannequin. Her green eyes stare at me; they have a blankness about them, as if they've been painted on her face. I wonder how she sees me? Does she see the baseball player in sweat pants and a Mets jacket, my baseball cap pushed well back on my head. Or am I just the guy who provided this air-conditioned living room, big as a furniture showroom. She really is comfortable here, all poise, self-assurance, and cool fingers. I wonder what became of the girl in the grey sweatshirt and blue jeans who used to bounce down the bleacher steps and hug my neck as I trotted in from the outfield when a game ended in any of a dozen sun-drenched small-town stadiums, during the years when I was in the minors.

"You know I can't," she says finally, turning her head toward me, looking at me as if she really loves me; maybe she believes she does. "It's just too much for Charlene to travel all the time, and mama's getting on . . ."

I stare quietly at her, picturing myself yelling, "You're in love with this damn glass and brick and carpet, the landscaped gardens, the odour of magnolia, the comfort, the quiet. You're repeating history, Gwen. Your mama drove off her husband and was left alone with you; now you're doing the same to me." I really want to say all that, but instead I turn away, resigned.

"If you're not coming with me, I may as well report to camp a few days early," I say. Gwen does not disagree with me.

I can see us at the airport, Gwen immaculate behind the wheel of the Lincoln as she stops next to the departure gate. I kiss Charlene, where she sits between us in her car seat; she coos, reaching her baby-fingers in my direction as if I were a bird or a butterfly.

"Where's your old lady?" one of the players will say to me when I offer to join them for a drink after our first practice.

"Barefoot and pregnant in Des Moines," I'll say, a little too loudly, though every word will hurt like needles passing through my lips.

The Firefighter

The Firefighter

It's Cal that I want to tell you about. But it seems there are so many other things I should get to first, like Delly and my baseball career. I just finished Rookie League up in Butte, Montana. The Butte Copper Kings. We finished 25-45 for the season, but I batted .337 and hit 30 homers in 70 games. Up in Montana winter breathes on you all year round; the grass was white with frost one morning before we left Butte on the last day of August.

It sure ain't cold where we are, headin' from Tulsa toward Oklahoma City, where we're gonna spend the off-season. The heat-gauge on this rattle-trap '71 Plymouth has gone clear out of sight and it must be a hundred outside the car. Delly's fanning her thighs with a baseball program from Kansas City, where we stopped off for three days to see how they play in the Bigs, a place where I'm gonna be in two, three years at the most. Delly grins and fans and don't mind lettin' me see there's a wet spot in the crotch of her denim cutoffs.

I'd pull off the road right now if there was anywhere to pull off to except sand dunes and red rock hot enough to fry steak. I know if I ever stop this rickety car it will just die and go to

Plymouth heaven right by the side of the road.

We ain't actually headin' for Oklahoma City, but for a place called El Reno: twenty-two adobe buildings, five service stations, and an air-conditioned Taco Bell. Thirty-five miles past El Reno, out in the sage brush, is where Delly's family lives. Cal is Delly's father and he's the one I want to tell you about. There's an oil-donkey about every hundred yards on Cal's land, turnin' slow in the desert glare like big birds primpin' themselves. Cal don't own the oil rights so he ain't gettin' rich, but the oil company pays him so much for each land site.

I should tell you more about Cal being a firefighter and all, but I can't help thinkin' about this morning in the Blue Velvet Motel in Tulsa ($12.95 for two, day sleepers welcome), and how I was reading that same baseball program Delly's fannin' her thighs with, when I look up to see Delly come out of the bathroom. She don't actually come out. She just stands in the doorway, naked from the waist up, her titties pointing at the ceiling like they see something up there that I don't. Delly's got hair the same colour as the red desert sand and it's kind of mussed and casual like she just crawled out of the sack, which she did. She's wearing faded blue jeans not quite done up and she's leanin' against the door jamb starin' at me with her big, sleepy-blue eyes in a way that makes me toss the program on the floor and polevault over to her. Before we know it the maid is knockin' on the door tellin' us it's noon and check-out time for us was eleven.

Now it's Cal, and Eddie, and Regina, and Ma, who are Delly's immediate family, that I want to tell you about, and how they live so far back in the boonies, that, as they say on TV documentaries, they've hardly been disturbed by time or sanity.

"You ain't quite what I expected, but I expect you'll do," is what Delly said to me after the first time we was together in the single bed in the room she rented a few blocks from the university in Oklahoma City, where I'd come on a baseball scholarship. Delly was waitin' tables at a little bar patronized mainly by students. "I took a job here 'cause I figured I'd meet me a doctor or lawyer or maybe a dentist, 'cause they make the big money. I been poor the first eighteen years of my life and that's about long enough," is what she said to me, after we made love that was so sweet I couldn't have even imagined it. If somebody'd said to me, "Tell me about your wildest fantasy," I couldn't have dreamed up nothin' half as good as what Delly and me did that night.

I remember Delly comin' up to my table to take my order. She was wearin' blue jeans and a top the colour of green tomatoes, and I wondered if her titties had as many freckles on them as her face and arms. And the sound of denim rubbin' together as she walked away made me so horny that when I paid for my beer I held on to the dollar until our hands touched and I said, "I sure would like to know you better." And she said, "Where you from?" And I said, "Iowa." And she said, "That's a big state." And I said, "I'm like a fellow I read about in a story once. I'm not *from* a place, just from *near* a place. And if you ever heard of Onamata, Iowa, that's the place I was raised nearest to."

"I never," she said, and she frowned when I told her I was a Phys. Ed. major studying on a baseball scholarship.

"I ain't gonna be no Phys. Ed. teacher with a beer belly and a lot of might've-beens," I told Delly. "You come out and watch me hit the ball and see if you don't agree," and I guess she did, 'cause we been together ever since, and hasn't it been great.

"You let me worry about the money, Sugar," is what Delly said to me, and I let her. She banked her salary and tips and we lived off my scholarship money. When I graduated in the spring and got drafted by Seattle and then loaned to Butte for a summer in Rookie League, Delly said we could afford to get married.

Ballplayers in Rookie League ain't supposed to drag along wives or girlfriends. The scout who signed me looked at me like I was a pervert when I said I wanted to bring my wife with me. He arranged for one one-way airline ticket from Oklahoma City to Butte. Baseball club tried to make me take room and board with some solid-citizen baseball fans who would look after my *well being* while I was in Butte. But Delly took care of things. She left two days before me on the bus and rented a two-bedroom basement suite. We took in one of the Panamanian outfielders to fill up that spare bedroom. Delly got a job waiting tables in a bar and she wasn't afraid to wear peek-a-boo blouses. "I can count your pussy-hairs through them jeans," I said to her one afternoon as she was getting ready for work.

"You bet you can," she smiled, "they're worth about a dollar each in tips. Look, Sugar, them drunkies are always gonna be tipping too much in sleazy bars and they'll never have a pot to piss in or a window to throw it outa. You just keep hittin' the long ball and let me worry about the money."

And you know what? We're comin' back to a condo all our own in a nice new building near downtown Oklahoma City. And the payments aren't any more than rent would be and Delly already rented the extra room to a student.

I've met Delly's family and except for her Ma they'd make a great study for an anthropologist. This big company found oil on Cal's land about fifteen years ago, and Cal ain't worked since, not that he ever worked before.

"Pa used to run what he called an Underground Auto Wrecking business," Delly told me. "That means he sold stolen car parts. I went with him once or twice when I was a kid. We'd cruise into Oklahoma City and Pa would park behind a night club. 'Folks who can afford to drink can afford to donate to our livelihood,' he always said. Pa could strip four wheels, the spare, a couple of headlights and sometimes a grille off a pick-up in under four minutes. I seen him detach a mirror or strip a radio in broad daylight on the main street in about the time it would take somebody to sneeze."

Oil company pays Cal for the use of his land; they also pay him a thousand a month to stay the hell out of their hair, which he don't. They even appointed him head firefighter, whatever the hell that is. Delly says she don't remember there ever being a fire in that particular field. And anyway they only gave him a shiny new fire-engine-red pick-up truck with two pretty small fire extinguishers on the back. But that don't stop Cal from talkin' and actin' like he was Red Adair. Actually, Cal and

Delly look a lot alike, only he's a man, about twenty-five years older and a hundred pounds heavier.

When they gave out looks and brains in Delly's family they clean missed Eddie and Regina, Eddie being her brother, who could be a basketball player if he knew what it was, and Regina being her sister, who looks like Eddie, poor Regina. Delly's Ma is the only other one in the family who has any sense. She should go around with a whip and a chair to keep the others in line.

We pull into the yard at Delly's folks' place. There's just a frame house that lists about three ways at once and ain't never seen a paintbrush even in its dreams, a couple of garages and out-buildings that list worse than the house, and about an acre of wrecked car bodies, used tires and faded appliances. The front of the house is hung with hub caps — when the sun shines you can see them glint like swords from a couple of miles away. That little red pick-up shines like an apple in front of the house. Delly goes directly inside to talk with Ma and Regina, while Cal walks around the truck and then around our shivering old Plymouth, kickin' tires as he goes, remarking on how shiny his truck is, puttin' his fingers on the hood of the Plymouth and pullin' them back quick, remarkin' on how it's a wonder such a wreck made it all the way from Montana and saying he'll give me fifty dollars for it if we ever want it taken off our hands. Delly says we can get four hundred dollars for a trade-in come January, when prices are low. Cal cracks us each a beer from a tub in the front yard that used to be Ma's washing machine until Cal tried to fix it. The beer bottle is wet but warm, and I figure Cal must have recently tried to fix Ma's refrigerator too.

I was all for buyin' a car, maybe a big one, with some of the money Delly had stashed away. "Cars depreciate. Land appreciates," she said to me. "We'll have a big car, Babe. You gotta hang in for a while." She was standin' by my chair and sort of kissin' at my ear while she was sayin' that. "You give me five years in the Bigs, and I'll see we own enough of Oklahoma City so's I never have to wait on another drunk and you don't have to take no job sellin' used cars the way them other retired ballplayers do." I can't fault that.

Cal's wearin' bib-overalls, a Minnesota Twins baseball cap with about eight ounces of oil worked into the crown and the bill, and for whatever damn reason, rubber boots that must have his feet broiled up to the colour of corned beef.

Cal eventually decides to take the shiny red pick-up truck and make a tour of the oilfield, "Just to be sure there ain't no dangerous situation developin' that I should know about." I beg off sayin' I've travelled enough for one day. When I get to the screen door I stop, for I hear Delly's voice rising: "What do you do with your money?" she says in exasperation.

"What do you mean?" says Ma.

"Look around you," yells Delly. "You got nothin' an' never *had* nothin'." I'd guess Delly has her left hand on her hip and her right hand open, palm up, sort of gesturing at the floor. That's exactly the way Cal stands when he's making a point. Delly'd be mad at me for a month if I ever pointed that out to her.

"I don't remember you ever goin' hungry," says Ma, her voice defensive.

"Hungry ain't the point," says Delly. "That oil company pays Cal a thousand a month up front and then rents the rig-sites, and he still sells lots of stolen parts . . ."

"Don't say that," says Ma in a harsh whisper. And I'd guess she's just looked at Regina, who must be sittin' on a kitchen chair, her hands folded in her lap, starin' off into space, her face blank as a dog's.

"Are you still pretendin' you don't know Cal steals anything that ain't bolted to the ground and a few things that are?"

"Your papa's a nice man . . ."

"I'm not sayin' he ain't nice. But he's thoughtless and shiftless and . . . and . . . why did you ever marry him?"

"Your papa has a winnin' smile," says Ma, with finality, as if her statement answers all the philosophical questions ever posed.

Delly huffs with indignation and bangs a handful of cutlery into the dishpan. "I'd like to manage your income for a few months; you'd be livin' in a nice place in Oklahoma City, and

Cal could use this dump for a parts shack, like he's always done anyway."

The last time we were here there was a stripped-down motorcycle under the kitchen table and about two dozen generators sittin' around on the living room floor like a convention of alien pets.

"Oh, we couldn't move from here," says Ma. "Cal's on duty as a firefighter, twenty-four hours a day."

"For God's sake, Ma. They gave him that truck so he'd stay away from the oil-donkeys and rigs and stop sellin' booze to the roughnecks."

"You're too hard on your pa . . ."

I bang the screen door to let them know I'm here. Delly huffs a couple more times, but doesn't say anything. The motorcycle's still under the table, but Cal's found it a friend since we were here last. There's a dismantled trailbike keepin' it company.

"Where's Eddie?" Delly asks. "He in jail yet, or just workin' toward it?"

"Eddie's been working part-time on the rigs," says Ma. "He's goin' into El Reno tomorrow to buy his first new-to-him car."

"I should'a known," sighs Delly.

"Let's head into El Reno," Cal says to me after supper. I sort of glance at Delly to see how she feels about it. She ain't exactly been friendly toward her pa. She slammed his plate down in front of him so hard that some of the yellow beans jumped about a foot in the air and a couple came down in his coffee. When Cal deposited about a half-pound of butter in the middle of his grits Delly made a bad face. Then she suggested in no uncertain terms that Cal should buy Ma a new fridge, washer, dryer, stove, a TV that works, and that he should clear all his damn stolen parts outa the house.

At that point Cal says directly to me, "You know, boy, when a man comes home from a hard day's firefightin' or playin' with a baseball, or whatever, he don't want to be bothered with no women's stuff, you know what I mean?''

I said I reckoned I did. Delly looked at me like she'd just lifted up a rock and seen me for the first time. I wished right away I hadn't said it, and got busy eatin' my pork chops. I like sugar on my grits.

I don't exactly say that I'm goin' along but when Cal gets up from the table, belches, and heads for the door, I follow him. ''Don't expect me to bail you out if you get in trouble,'' says Delly.

''I'll be fine,'' I say.

''As long as you know you're in bad company,'' she says.

''Pussywhipped,'' says Cal as he guides the car across the desert, spirals of red dust coiling out behind us. ''Ain't nothin' worse than a pussywhipped man,'' he mumbles. ''If she'd said you can't go, you wouldn't be here.''

I don't deny it, which don't please Cal very much.

''Don't take no crap from 'em, boy. She's my own little girl, but I don't know where she gets off bein' so feisty.''

The Last Stand is located in a Quonset hut, surrounded by oilfield supply businesses on the far outskirts of El Reno. The building has one small window in the front, with two blue neon Coors signs bleeding down it. Inside there's a long bar down one wall and about twenty tables with scruffy kitchen chairs pushed under them, and a pool table at the very rear with one bright light above it.

''Bring us a coupla Coors and keep 'em comin','' Cal says and then he proceeds to tell anyone who cares to listen and a few who don't that he is the man taught Red Adair all about fightin' oilwell fires.

After about the third beer he spots a baseball sittin' on a shelf behind the bar. ''Stanley here is a pro-fessional baseball player,'' he says real loud, and slaps my shoulder, practically makin' me bust a tooth on my beer bottle.

''Lefty,'' I say. ''Nobody's called me Stanley since I started holdin' my baby bottle in my left hand.''

''Bet that wasn't the only thing you used to hold in your left hand,'' laughs Cal.

''I reckon it wasn't,'' I say, and laugh with him.

''Where y'all play?'' asks one of the roughnecks.

"Triple A," says Cal. "An All Star, goin' to be in the Bigs next season, you see if he ain't."

"What Triple A?" asks the roughneck.

"Hawaii," I say, not missin' a beat, and pickin' the team farthest away from Oklahoma City.

"Seen 'em three times in Honolulu this summer an' I don't remember you."

"I was out with an injury for about six weeks. Must of been then," I say. With my luck he'll have seen me in Butte, and remember me.

Cal winks at me, gathers up a handful of empty Coors bottles and walks to the end of the bar. He sets three of the squat empties at about one foot intervals on the end of the bar. The empties are about the same colour as the bar-wood and in the bad light they blend right in.

"I'm bettin'," says Cal, "that Stanley here can knock them three bottles off with three pitches of the ball," and he nods to where the baseball sits like a white tomato beside the cash register.

"Cal," I whisper, "how many people here know your full name is Calvin Washington Jefferson Coolidge Collinwood?"

"I'm bettin' my son-in-law, Lefty here . . ." and he repeats the proposition, flashing a wad of twenties.

"I'll take fifty," says one roughneck.

"Twenty says he can't hit three outa three," growls a guy built like a jeep, and with enough oil on his clothes to soak down a quarter mile of red dust.

"I ain't sure I can do it," I whisper to Cal.

"Cal here ain't never rowed with but one oar in the water," says the bartender, winking at me. "I'll take fifty of that."

"Put your money away," I whisper to Cal. "I ain't a pitcher."

"Hell, boy, you play way out there in the outfield, you told me so yourself. You got to throw two, three times as far as a pitcher. Can't be no more'n forty feet from one end of this bar to the other." And he waves the roll of bills again. "Duck soup," he says.

There's about $250 dollars riding on my arm. The bartender tosses me the baseball. "You know," he says, "one time

Mickey Mantle came in here. Was just drivin' past, but the fellow drivin' Mick's 1956 scarlet Lincoln Continental convertible was sailin' her at about 125 mph. The sheriff hauled them over, but he brought them here instead of to jail. Mick bought a round for the house and he signed a baseball. It said, 'Best wishes to Sheriff McCall and everybody at the Last Stand,' and it was signed 'Your Friend, Mickey Mantle.' But somebody stole it right off the back of the bar.''

They discuss whether I should get warm-up pitches or not and decide against it. It is awkward as hell to wind-up indoors, and I can barely see them little brown bottles at the far end of the bar. I let drive at the one on the left and hit the centre one dead on, sendin' it screamin' across the top of the pool table where it shatters against the back wall. All the people have been moved out of that part of the bar so it don't do no damage. There must be fifty people standin' around watchin' me.

I let fly at the left one again, and the ball bounces off the bar about two feet in front of the bottle but rises just enough to tip the rim, and the bottle topples off the bar.

"I told you he was a pro-fessional," says Cal. "He might even pitch this one from behind his back.''

I give Cal one mean stare; he catches my drift and shuts up.

I take a big stretch and wing one at the last bottle. There's a stitch loose in the baseball from ricochetin' around the bar after my other pitches, and it makes a whirrin' sound and curves way more than I ever intended it to. Still it only misses to the right by about two inches.

"I be go to hell," says Cal, as people rush up to collect their bets. Somebody retrieves the ball and the bartender hands it to me, along with a pen. I sign it, 'Best Wishes to everybody at the Last Stand, your friend Lefty Brooks.'

"I need me some fresh air," says Cal, headin' for the side door. "I be go to hell," he's mumblin'. "Shoulda bet 'em two out of three.''

"Cal keeps the whole town in spendin' money," says the bartender, grinning. "Brought in this little spit-lizzard one day an' took bets he could eat it alive . . .''

After about ten minutes I figure I need some air too.

As I head out the side door I hear a little chink-chink sound off to my left. The moon looks like a slice of silver floatin' on its back in the sky.

"Pssst," says a voice that I know is Cal's.

I walk into the darkness to where there are five or six cars parked. Cal is just lettin' down his jack and the pick-up truck he's been workin' on is level to the sand. A wheel lays flat on its side beside where each axle rests on the ground.

"Give us a hand here," says Cal, pickin' up one of them wheels and layin' it on my outstretched arms. Then he stacks another wheel on top of the first one. "Take 'em to the truck," he whispers. "I'm gonna get me the grille and the front bumper."

I am only about halfway to the truck when a car switches on its lights, and I feel like a convict getting picked up by a search-light beam.

"Just stay right where you are," says a voice behind the light.

I do. There are footsteps comin' up behind me on the red shale. "Now where'd you get that armful of wheels," says the voice.

"Would you believe I won them from this guy in the bar?" I say. The voice steps around where I can see it, and it belongs to a man in a sheriff's uniform who is way taller than I am, wearin' a trooper's hat, and packin' a gun and a badge.

"Don't set 'em down," says the sheriff, noticin' my knees beginnin' to buckle under the weight. "Just carry these here wheels back into the Stand and we'll check out your story."

I take a couple of steps toward the bar before I have second thoughts. The wheels almost certainly belong to one of the roughnecks. Those dudes are so tough even their spit has muscles. And most of them have some pretty primitive ideas of justice. I figure I could be in a lot worse company.

"I was plannin' to pay for them when I could," I say.

"I'm sure you were, son. Now where did you put the jack?"

"I didn't use one," I say, settin' the wheels down and breathin' heavily.

"You reckon you can put them back without a jack?"

"No sir. They's easier to take off than put on."

The sheriff walks to the back of the black-and-white and opens the trunk. "Take out the jack," he says to me. "I don't want to get my hands dirty. I'll move the cruiser over and give you some light to work by, then I'll just write this up while you put the wheels back on."

While he's moving the patrol car I notice Cal's truck easin' off the lot and straight out into the desert, no sign of lights about it.

The sheriff stands with a foot on the bumper of the patrol car and writes on a clipboard, while I sweat the wheels into place and tighten the lug nuts.

"You come into town with Junkyard Cal, right?"

"Eeeyuh," I say, hoping the sound can be interpreted as either yes or no.

"All the way from Iowa, eh?" he says looking at my driver's licence. "You must be the guy married Cal's good-lookin' daughter?"

"Eeeyuh," I say again.

"If I thought you were dumb enough to be courtin' the other one, I'da probably shot ya for a stray. That Regina Collinwood is the ugliest girl in six counties; she is gonna be a burden to Cal in his old age. There ain't much goes on around El Reno that I don't know about," the sheriff goes on. "Cal's not really a bad man. He usually steals from strangers, or at least people who can afford it. He sells reasonable, and his initiative keeps him off the county welfare."

At the jail the sheriff lets me wash-up before he locks me in the second of two cells. The first one is occupied by a forlorn-looking Mexican who's playing "The Streets of Laredo" on a plastic harmonica.

"We'll just wait for a while and see who comes to fetch you," says the sheriff, grinning. "I hope it's Cal. Doggone, but I love to listen to Cal lie. Ain't nobody in these parts can do it better. I sure would like to know how he talked that oil company into givin' him that truck."

"Ain't I allowed a phone call?" I ask the sheriff.

"Call me Bud," he says, "an' sure, you're allowed a phone call; but who you figurin' on callin'? I reckon there ain't no phone out at Cal's place, unless'n he's tapped in on the oil company line again. Did that a year or two ago, but they got a little testy when he charged up a couple of thousand dollars' worth of long-distance bills. He was sellin' his car parts in about forty states there for a while."

I guess he can see I'm lookin' kind of worried.

"Also, if I let you use the phone I got to read you your rights, an' if I do that I got to book you, an' if I do that why things can get plumb out of my control, and you never can tell what might happen. So why don't we just wait around until somebody comes to get you. I suspect Cal will come pussyfootin' in like a coyote casing a hen house. Doggone, I never did look at the front of that truck; did he get the grille?"

"I don't know, sir."

"Magnets for fingers, that's what Cal's got. They should have a contest for strippin' down cars on *Real People* or *That's Incredible*. Cal could become a genuine celebrity if they did. Why don't you catch forty winks, boy. And let me give you a little advice: if you gonna steal, don't be dumb enough to get caught."

It wasn't Cal come to get me.

About 5:00 a.m. I hear the brakes on the '71 Plymouth singing from about a quarter mile away as Delly starts slowin' her down. The sheriff gets up from his desk and goes out to meet her.

"You holdin' Lefty here?"

"Sure am," says the sheriff.

"How much is he gonna cost me?"

"How much you figure you can afford?"

"Don't be cute. I just want to bail him out."

"You go have a word with him while I figure out the charges," he says.

Delly starts talkin' as she crosses into the room. "I woke up with a start about four o'clock and you wasn't there and I could hear Cal snorin' so I knew somethin' was wrong." All I can think of is how good she looks to me. She's missed the bottom button on her blouse so it's done up crooked all the way, and her red-rock hair is all tousled, one leg of her jeans is pushed into her boot the other is caught on the top and bunched up. She must wonder why I'm grinnin' as if I just hit a home run with a big-league scout watchin'. "I had to thump on Cal for about five minutes before he woke up. 'Where's Lefty?' I yelled. 'He got himself in a mite of trouble,' said Cal. 'Why didn't you tell me,' I screamed. 'You was sleepin' when I come in, and he'll still be there in the morning. I figured we'd all drive to town bright an' early, and I'd treat for breakfast at the Pronghorn Drive-in after we picked him up.' 'What'd he do?' I asked. 'Well, I don't rightly know,' said Cal. 'You know how these young fellas is, always lettin' off steam.' So what did you do? And what did Cal have to do with it?''

"I sort of got in a fight," I say. "This here cowboy mistook you for your sister and said I was married to the ugliest girl in six counties. Now I couldn't stand for that, could I?"

"I woulda bet money Cal was involved some way. Is he tellin' the truth?" she says to the sheriff.

"Yes, ma'am, he is," says the sheriff, and I breathe easy.

"Well, how much is the fine?"

"I reckon he's cooled down by now. I'll just let him off with time in custody. You take him home, Miss Delores, and take good care of him. I expect to see him in the Big Leagues next year. Y'all remember me to your papa, ya hear?"

The next day Delly ain't exactly happy with me or Cal. But, oddly enough, her anger kind of draws Cal and me together.

I guess Cal is a little sheepish about runnin' out on me, because he ain't got around to mentioning last night at all. We make a lot of small talk about the weather. Eventually he goes and digs for a while in a big metal box that has *Gulf Oil* stencilled on the side of it, and comes sidling over to me, one hand behind his back.

"I won this from a guy in a pool game a few years back," he says, producing a baseball. "You bein' a pro-fessional and all I thought you might appreciate it."

The baseball is brown and dry as if it's been baked in an oven. The inscription is still visible — "Your Friend, Mickey Mantle."

"I do appreciate it, Cal," I say. "I'll put it right on top of the TV in our new condo."

We are still makin' small talk and suckin' beer when we see a cloud of red dust puffin' up behind the closest sand ridge and a strange car comes barrelin' into the yard, screams straight through the chickens, and spins around with so much noise it brings Ma and Regina out onto the sloping wooden porch. When the dust settles downwind, givin' Cal and me a faceful, Delly's brother Eddie unwinds from behind the wheel and stands there like a smilin' hairpin.

"I be go to hell," says Cal, and then to me, "it's Eddie with his new-to-him car."

Eddie just stands grinnin' at us through the hole in his face where he got two teeth knocked out in a Chicano bar up to El Reno. We all walk around the car, which is a '57 or '8 Buick of a kind of winey-red colour, like we were doing some kind of ritual. We kick the three whitewalls and one regular tire and comment on how great she looks. I mean, what else can you say to a guy that's just got his first new-to-him car, except that it looks good, even if it's covered in dents and got about the same number of rods knocking, and has tailfins on which you could terminally injure yourself.

"Looks like she's puckered to shit," says Cal. And I know that Cal still likes to come home with a new-to-him car and take everybody for a ride into El Reno, where he parks in the Taco Bell lot right outside the dining room window. Then everybody goes inside where it's downright cold, orders Mexican food, and grins at the car through the thick, polished glass.

Eddie hops behind the wheel, kind of folding himself up like he was made of coathangers, taking two or three tries to get all of him into the car. Eddie was six-foot-eight the last time anybody measured him, which was a couple of years ago when he was in his third year of Grade 8.

"Ain't this just the best shitkickin' car you ever laid eyes on?" Eddie wants to know. And nobody's about to tell him it ain't true.

"Maaaa," he bawls, "come for a ride." Then he hollers for Delores to get on out of the house and see his new car, and for Regina to be careful as hell of the leopard-skin seat covers when she gets in the back seat.

"Come on, guys?" he says to us.

"Can't," says Cal. "I'm on duty." He says this with both thumbs hooked over the straps of his overalls.

"Ain't gonna be no *fire*," says Eddie.

"Never can tell," says Cal.

"You catch me next trip," says Delly, after she's admired the colour of the paint and the big plastic statue of Jesus on a spring that's held to the dashboard by a suction cup.

As soon as Ma closes the passenger door Eddie takes off spinnin' the wheels and scatterin' the chickens again. The force of his start tips Regina over backwards from where she was hangin' onto the back of the passenger seat.

After the dust settles Cal cracks us each another warm beer. Delly's gone in the house and I bet to the back bedroom that used to be hers. I remember that first night in Oklahoma City when Delly took me to her room. When I started to take her clothes off she helped me, and things have been gettin' better ever since. I'm kind of sidl'n toward the house but Cal is busy tellin' me all the things he knows about, like cam shafts and oil rigs. I let my mind wander until I hear him say something about, "What you reckon that is over yonder?"

When I open my eyes I see a streak of smoke risin' on the horizon. "Maybe it's an oilwell fire?" I say.

Cal looks at me like I was Eddie or Regina.

"Oilwells go BOOM, and shoot fire way up into the air, and any goddamned oilwell firefighter knows that," shouts Cal.

"You're the expert," I tell him.

"What's over the hill is likely only a brush fire," says Cal, then he goes on to tell me how Red Adair blasted sea water into the Big One in Alaska in '73. And he woulda told me about the whole ten days Adair worked on that run-away oilwell if I hadn't pointed out that someone is coming running up the road.

"I be go to hell," says Cal, "they is movin' right along."

"It's Ma," I say, 'cause I can see further than Cal even when he squints. "We better hop in the truck and go meet her."

"No use gettin' excited over nothin'," says Cal. "Let's just wait and see what she's got to say for herself." Cal is still squintin' down the road and is about ready to believe me that it's Ma runnin' toward us. Cal is rollin' a cigarette real careful, and asks me to fetch him another beer while he is strikin' a wooden match on the seat of his overalls.

Ma is yellin' at the top of her lungs. And as she gets closer we can hear that it's all about Eddie and his new-to-him car.

"Burnin', burnin' up," is what Ma is gasping. Then, "Couldn't you guys see me comin'? Why didn't you come meet me?"

"We didn't know for sure it was anything serious," says Cal. "Y'all just keep calm; you're in the company of a professional firefighter." All three of us are in the shiny red pick-up truck and Cal manages to do just about half a wheelie as we screech out of the yard, scattering them bedraggled chickens again. I'm pretty sure I seen Delly peeking out one of the curtainless windows as we roar away.

Sure enough, about a mile down the road, just overtop the first rise, is Eddie's car, hood up, burnin' like a spit-cat.

"I be go to hell," says Cal, as he swings down outa his truck and walks slowly around the burnin' car.

Eddie is bellowin' like a young moose that just lost its mama. "Where the hell you bin? Put out the fire!" and other stuff like that.

"I'm the firefighter around here," says Cal, climbin' up and takin' one of the shiny silver fire extinguishers off the back of the truck cab.

"Red Adair always takes his time," Cal says, trying to decide the best angle to shoot the flames. Cal gets all set, his boots braced as if he expects the extinguisher to kick like a rifle.

"Let her rip," shouts Cal, and pulls the handle on the extinguisher.

"Pffffft," says the extinguisher, and drops a couple of globs of foam on the road.

"I be go to hell," says Cal, and looks kind of puzzled.

Eddie is bellowin' so loud that if he'd do it on the fire he might put it out.

Regina just stands in the ditch wringin' her hands, and it's a good place for her 'cause she don't look anywhere near her six-foot-two standin' in the ditch.

And Ma, who's been watchin' cars burn up for thirty years, knows better than to say anything at all.

Cal heads back for the truck, mumbling about Red Adair always being prepared for any emergency. Somehow I see kind of a combination of Cal and Red Adair in a pair of Boy Scout shorts, and I laugh like hell.

Cal gives me a look like I just shit in one of his boots. He is up in the box of the pick-up trying to wrestle the second fire extinguisher loose from the truck. The extinguisher has a mind of its own. Cal gets both his pudgy hands around that extinguisher as if he was stranglin' it, and he braces his boots against the back of the cab and pulls with all his 225 pounds. Finally the extinguisher lets go and Cal crashes down on his back in the truck box and the extinguisher sails over his head and lands with a thunk in the dust.

Eddie pounces on it as quick as Eddie can pounce on anything, grabs it up, points it in the general direction of his burnin' car and fires it. It shoots like a dammer. Only the foam swishes right overtop of the car and hits Regina at about the spot where her boobies might be, if she had any.

"Looks like a cat just fell in the separator bowl," says Cal, picking himself up and relieving Eddie of the extinguisher.

"Gimme that thing, boy. Let a professional firefighter handle this."

Cal finally gets the foam pointed in the right direction. When he's finished the car looks like it's been sittin' in a blizzard for a week. It's totalled. After it's cooled off, me and Cal and Eddie push it into the ditch. Eddie is crying. And even Cal gives him a sympathetic slap on the shoulder. I mean you got to feel somethin' for a guy has just had his first new-to-him car burn up on the side of the road.

"Let's all go into town for a beer just the way regular oil-field firefighters do," says Cal. If Eddie'll stop cryin' Cal will let him drive the shiny red pick-up truck, providin' he promises to keep it on the road. "You can even have all the burritos you can eat at Taco Bell,'' offers Cal.

All four of them cram into the cab of that pick-up. I beg off ridin' in the truck box saying I'll just walk back to the house and keep Delly company. I figure by now she'll be over being mad about last night.

The Battery

The Battery

It was during the sixth month of his mother's pregnancy that, inside her belly, Esteban Cortizar began to throw the sidearm curve.

"Yi! Yi!" screamed Fernandella Cortizar, as Esteban went into the stretch, hiding the ball carefully in his glove so the batter could not glimpse the way he gripped it.

"Yiii!" shrilled Fernandella, as Esteban's arm snaked like a whip in the direction of third base, while the ball, travelling the path of a question mark, jug-hooked its way to the plate, and smacked into a catcher's mitt held by Esteban's twin brother Julio.

Many years later, on her deathbed, Fernandella Cortizar, wizened and gray with age, attended by servants, small as a child in the queen-sized bed in the marble-pillared mansion her sons had built for her, recalled the time of her pregnancy. She was residing on the outskirts of Santo Domingo, in a cardboard hut with a precariously balanced slab of corrugated tin for a roof. The hovel was located on an arid sidehill, surrounded by a few prickly vines, always in full view of the frying sun. Her husband, a sly young man with slicked-down hair, drooping eyelids, and a face thin as a ferret's, spent his life at the baseball grounds, winning or losing a few pesos on the outcome of each day's games. He was proud of Fernandella's belly, which by the fourth month was big as a washtub, forcing her to walk splay-legged as she trekked out each morning in search of fresh water and fresh fruit.

When she first told her husband she was pregnant he took her to see a wizard who lived in a tent near the baseball grounds.

"If he is such a wizard why isn't he rich, or President of the Republic, or both?" Fernandella cried.

The wizard, Jorge Blanco, existed by predicting the outcome of baseball matches. In the mornings, a steady stream of gamblers made their way to his tent, paying five centavos for each prophesy. The wizard never gambled himself, and hedged his prognostications. Unless a game seemed a sure thing, he advised half the gamblers to bet one side, and half to bet the other, swearing each side to secrecy.

As a child, the wizard had stowed away on a rum-running boat and had spent two whole days in Miami, where he had seen a hot-air balloon. The moment he had seen it rise from the earth, hissing like a million snakes, he knew the feel of magic, and he realized his rôle in life was to be a wizard. It was the first time he had ever experienced wonder. His second exposure to wonder occurred the same afternoon when he stumbled on a Major League baseball team engaged in spring training, and discovered that professional baseball players were well paid, well fed, and overly respected.

"Twins," the wizard proclaimed proudly, pressing the newly taut skin on Fernandella's belly. "Twin sons." The inside of the wizard's tent was stifling and smelled of fruit rinds and stale clothing.

Fernandella's husband beamed; Fernandella scowled at the wizard. "How much is this going to cost?" she demanded.

"Twin sons who will be great, no, not just great, but two of the greatest baseball players ever to originate in the Dominican Republic," the wizard went on, ignoring Fernandella.

The wizard lived in poverty in a tent made of stolen canvas, saving his money to someday acquire a hot-air balloon. He planned then to fly like a bird over the Dominican Republic, sizzling down out of the sky as a wizard ought to, his own costume made of parrot-bright silks, contrasting with the sleek brilliance of the balloon.

"That will be fifteen centavos," he said to Fernandella's husband.

"Thief," said Fernandella, watching her husband dig in the pocket of his ragged trousers. It was at that moment she felt the first painful stirrings in her belly: though she could not comprehend the nature of the pain, and did not know it was caused by a pitcher gouging out dirt in front of the pitcher's rubber, making a place for his forward foot to land comfortably.

"Eyyya," groaned Fernandella, grasping her belly with one sepia-coloured hand.

"To be completely fair," said the wizard to Fernandella's husband, "I will prophesy the outcome of three baseball games of your choice, for the same ridiculously low fee."

The birth of Esteban and Julio Cortizar was the wizard's first triumph. He lurked like a jackal in the dry weeds behind the shack while the births were taking place. The wizard's eyes glistened while his skin shone like polished teakwood.

The father appeared once to announce: "The first one was born in the catcher's crouch. His little hands are already scarred. He has suffered several broken knuckles."

The wizard, lean as a coyote, rubbed his thin hands together and decided henceforth he would call himself Alfredo Jorge Blanco.

"The second one, the one we will christen Esteban, was born wearing baseball cleats," the father announced with wicked pride the next time he returned to the thicket. The wizard was dressed in an ink-blue robe covered with mysterious symbols. "The fingers on his pitching hand are like talons, the first two fingers splayed, the nails sharpened to fierce points."

"Did I not prophesy so?" asked the wizard, Alfredo Jorge Blanco, trying not to show his astonishment, his mind whirling as he tried to decide how best to exploit the situation.

After the births, after the midwife had swaddled Esteban and Julio in blankets made from freshly laundered sugar sacks, after she stretched Julio out of his catcher's crouch, and attempted to force Esteban to lay like a baby and stop the continual pitching motions, she propped the babies, one on each side of Fernandella, their tiny maple faces each resting against a swollen breast. It was then the midwife discovered that, along with the twins, Fernandella's womb had expelled two miniature baseball gloves, one a catcher's mitt, three kumquat-sized baseballs, and a pen-sized bat. If Esteban was the pitcher and Julio the catcher, who held the bat was never known.

Soon after the baseball-playing twins were born, a clear brook, four inches wide, with water the cold blue of ice, began flowing down the hill, passing only yards from the tin-roofed shack. The stream plashed softly and the cool waters held a plentiful supply of irridescent parrot-fish, their larkspur-blue bodies darting like shadows. A guava tree in full fruition appeared among the bone-dry scrub on the hillside behind the shack, where the wizard had skulked. A dozen lemon-crested cockatoos appeared in a row on the tin roof and kept the area free from insects, while the yard filled with pheasants and game hens, tame as puppies, anxious to lay down their lives to provide food for Fernandella and her family.

The babies slept at the opposite ends of their crib, each in their accustomed positions: Estaban as if he had just delivered a sidearm curve, Julio as if he had just caught one.

By six months of age the twins were playing catch with passionfruit. Esteban was long and lean with an oval face and high forehead, while Julio was stocky and wide-faced with a low hairline and tea cup ears.

At two years of age Esteban struck out his father, using two curve balls and a sinking slider. For their first birthday, Salvador Alfredo Jorge Blanco, as the wizard now called himself, built a pitcher's mound beside the stream where the blue fish darted like needles. The wizard supplemented his income by charging the gamblers ten centavos apiece to hide behind the guava tree and watch the battery practice, for Fernandella had forbidden her husband or the wizard to make any profit from her remarkable children.

Fernandella's husband saw to it that she became pregnant again as quickly as possible, in fact she produced four more children at ten month intervals, two boys and two girls. The wizard made no predictions over Fernandella's newly taut belly, though her husband beseeched him to; the wizard even declined to predict the sex of the unborn. To the great disappointment of Fernandella's husband the children were all without abnormalities.

Word of the miraculous baseball-playing babies travelled outward from the Dominican Republic on the rum-running boats. In neighbouring Haiti, Papa Doc Duvalier, when he heard of the astonishing children, sent an emissary with golf-ball sized diamonds on his ebony fingers, who offered to buy the babies from their father in return for a ten pound bar of gold and six virgins. In Haiti, women who had had sex only with Papa Doc Duvalier were still considered virgins. On the advice of the wizard, Fernandella's husband turned down the offer.

"The gold bar has a leaden centre and the virgins have the pox," said the wizard, who had bigger plans for the battery. In America he knew, baseball players were rich and much worshipped. They were admired more than generals, bullfighters, plantation owners, or even Papa Doc Duvalier.

As the twins grew older Fernandella's vigilance slackened. Overwhelmed with newer babies and perpetual pregnancy she eventually became relieved to see the twins troop off with their father and the wizard in the direction of the baseball fields. By the time they were five they were playing in a league for teenagers and winning regularly. Their father became almost prosperous by betting on them, until bookmakers refused to accept any more bets on the battery of Esteban and Julio.

By the time the boys were seven years old they were playing in the best league in the Dominican Republic and were virtually unbeatable. The wizard laboriously wrote a letter which he addressed to:

El Presidente
American State of Miami
The World

Since he mistrusted the Dominican Postal Service, the wizard sent the letter to America by rum-runner. He signed the letter: Umberto Salvador Alfredo Jorge Blanco.

The letter, by a highy circuitous route, found its way to the Governor of Florida, who, having ambitions to be at least a senator, if not President, forwarded it to the owner of the Washington Senators Baseball Club. If he was eventually to live in Washington, the governor decided, he would like the Senators to at least be competitive in the American League. The last time they had had a winning season was in 1952, the time before that 1945; they had not won a pennant since 1933, and had won their last, and only World Series in 1924.

At the time, with the breaking of the colour ban fairly recent history, major league teams were just beginning to seriously scout the baseball players of the Dominican Republic, Panama, Puerto Rico, and the like.

The Washington Senators sent a scout to Santo Domingo. The scout was a famous baseball star of the twenties, who had more losing battles with the bottle than anyone cared to remember. After seeing the battery of Esteban and Julio in action he stayed sober for two full weeks, just to be certain that what he was witnessing was real.

Esteban Cortizar is the best baseball pitcher I have ever seen, he wrote back, but he is only eight years old. What do I do? Can I sign him? Can I sign his father? He has an agent of sorts, a man in a blue silk dress that has silver stars, crescents, triangles and hammers all over it. How soon do you think we can introduce this boy into organized baseball? Aren't there child labour laws to contend with? Or would something like this fall under the Coogan Law? By the way, Esteban pitches to his twin brother, who is an average catcher but who can't hit the plate with his bat. I understand they come as a pair, because the pitcher won't let anyone else catch him.

The owner of the Washington Senators was on intimate terms with the President of the United States. In fact, the President had once suggested to the Leader of the House, in a not altogether joking manner, that the House Leader should introduce a bill to break up the New York Yankees. The President indicated that he would be happy to sign such a bill into law.

The President and the owner of the Washington Senators conferred deep into the night.

The Senators signed the father of the twins to a two year contract as a scout. Though the father never realized it, he was paid more as a scout than the manager of the Senators.

The Senators also offered to rent the family a comfortable home in a pleasant district of Santo Domingo. However, Fernandella refused to leave the cool stream full of flashing fish, the shady guava tree, the yardful of docile pheasants who did everything but pluck and eviscerate themselves so anxious were they to grace Fernandella's table. Reluctantly, and at great cost, for the wizard somehow managed to become general contractor, the Senators had a home built on the sidehill, complete with a basement holding an electric furnace. The plans for the house were drawn up by a Minneapolis firm with a Federal Consulting Contract.

The Washington Senators, in consultation with the President of the United States, decided they would wait until Esteban was ten years old before signing him. Deep in the bowels of the Capitol, the U.S. Government Printing Office manufactured birth certificates for Esteban and Julio showing them to be sixteen years of age.

The bonus Esteban's father demanded for signing was a hot-air balloon. The Senators complied, for their negotiators were vaguely intimidated by the sinister demeanor of the wizard, who seemed always present, his silks swishing malevolently in the background. They knew the hot-air balloon was for the wizard and they hoped it would encourage him to travel extensively. The wizard, though he did not actually take part in the deal-making, was inclined to take the negotiators for a walk along the yard-wide, crystal stream full of blue fish sparkling like quicksilver; the wizard made the negotiators aware that the stream began from nothing and diminished to nothing, and while he never claimed responsibility; he intimated strongly that he had something to do with its emergence.

The twins, the day after their tenth birthday, armed with their official birth certificates, left Santo Domingo on an airplane bound for the mysterious United States, where, they had been told, baseball players were revered as gods.

To their right, as they took off, loomed the balloon of the wizard: the balloon was made of alternating stripes of cardinal-red and enamel-white, while in the gondola, waving animatedly, floated the wizard in his gown of blue and silver.

Esteban won sixteen games and lost four in his first season and was named Rookie of the Year in the American League. Julio batted .196 and was allowed to catch only when Esteban pitched. The Senators still finished last, the quality of the remainder of the team was so questionable that most of the players would have trouble playing first-string in Triple A baseball.

Back in Santo Domingo, the boy's father gambled with abandon. The wizard, who now called himself Cayetano Umberto Salvador Alfredo Jorge Blanco, ordered a second hot-air balloon.

Asked by the *St. Louis Sporting News* why he did not accompany the twins to Washington, the wizard replied, "The United States is not conducive to angels."

Esteban and Julio, after viewing the White House, decided that they wanted their mother to live there, in fact they made it a condition of their playing a third season in Washington. It did not matter to them when the Senators waved signed contracts under their noses and threatened to suspend them and let them rot in Santo Domingo, and never play another major league game. The twins pointed out, through their interpreter, a cousin of the wizard, that the baseball stadium was full for every home game, though the Senators continued to finish dead last. They pointed out that the previous year Esteban had won twenty-seven of the Senator's sixty-two victories.

The President of the United States agreed that Fernandella

Cortizar, and her children, who now numbered seven, all unexceptional, could visit the White House, even stay for a few days, two weeks at maximum, as guests of the State Department. The Cortizar brothers found a Spanish-speaking travel agent and booked first class seats to Santo Domingo. "We already have enough money to live comfortably forever in the Dominican Republic," they told the Senators.

The first time the battery returned home they paraded their money like military medals. They bought their mother silk dresses of irridescent greens and silvers; they bought her scarves and jewellery. On that first visit the brothers discovered that many of their neighbours, at the instigation of the wizard, were worshipping the furnace in the basement of Fernandella's house. It was the only furnace in all the Dominican Republic. The local priest refused to bless it, claiming it was an instrument of the devil; the wizard conversed with it. Fernandella's children, and Fernandella herself felt comforted by the way it hummed like a sleeping pet in the black hours before dawn.

The twins told Fernandella they wanted to buy her a villa on the sea in the richest section of Santo Domingo. Fernandella refused to leave her stream-of-plenty; she still killed pheasants for each family meal. It was the endless supply of fish and the pheasants that all but leapt into her frying pan that saved the day for the Washington Senators. Fernandella refused to even visit the United States.

"If the President wishes to see me so badly let him come here," said Fernandella. As for seeing her sons play professional baseball, she said simply, "Watching my sons play baseball brings back painful memories."

The twins hired an architect who reconstructed the White House on the barren, sun-scorched hillside on the outskirts of Santo Domingo. The replica was built in such a way that the magic stream splashed through the rose garden.

Esteban and Julio were exceptionally generous with their father. They gave him a large allowance which he gambled away. The wizard was now the biggest bookmaker in all Santo Domingo. The only client he dealt with personally was the father of the twins. For 101 consecutive days Esteban and

Julio's father bet on losing teams. The wizard, who never asked directly for anything from the twins, became a very wealthy man. He became interested in overthrowing the government. He acquired a fleet of hot-air balloons.

For each of the next three seasons Esteban won thirty games or more for the Senators. Each year the team finished above .500 and by developing a young and talented outfield, were in a position to win a pennant. In February, just before he was due to report for spring training in Florida, Esteban Cortizar was kidnapped by the Dominican guerillas, who at one time had been the government, and would be again. The government would then become the guerillas and the cycle would repeat itself.

The guerillas first demanded, in return for Esteban's safe release, money and arms from the Government of the Dominican Republic.

"Why should we care about the safety of a mere baseball player, who is fast becoming a gringo," replied the government. "Do with him as you will."

"You do not understand," the guerillas replied. "In the United States baseball players of quality are revered as saints. If the United States deems your government responsible for the death of Esteban Cortizar, it could result in diminished foreign aid. Since it is a well known fact that you use all agricultural and social service foreign aid money for military equipment, then where would you be?"

"We will take our chances," the government replied.

The kidnapping made the front pages of the *Washington Post* and the *St. Louis Sporting News*.

The wizard, Cayetano Umberto Salvador Alfredo Jorge Blanco, volunteered to seek out the guerillas and act as an intermediary.

The guerillas said they would shoot down his balloon on sight.

The wizard promised to make himself invisible.

The Washington Senators offered the guerillas five hundred dollars, no questions asked, for the return of Esteban Cortizar.

The guerillas set an execution date.

"I will pay you one-quarter of my salary and all the residuals from my Jalapena Bean Dip commercials," Esteban told the guerillas, some of whom were his childhood friends. When they rejected the offer he promised to buy all the guns in the largest pawn shop in Miami and ship them to the guerillas by rum-runner.

Preceded only by an eerie hissing of calamitous magnitude, the wizard appeared suddenly in the middle of the guerilla fortress. He was freshly shaved and manicured, dressed in velvet breeches and knee-high boots.

"I will buy uniforms for all the guerilla officers," he said. With his long, pale fingers he withdrew coloured pens from the ears of the officers present, and sketched uniforms of turquoise fabric, spangled with gold braid and flamingo-coloured epaulets, which quickened the hearts of the kidnappers. "Picture yourselves dressed thusly, marching in triumph into Santo Domingo," whispered the wizard who knew the secret desires of every man with whom he came in contact.

"Perhaps you would care to join our fight for freedom?" said the guerilla leader, who knew the wizard's secret desire.

The guerillas postponed the execution for two weeks. Cayetano Umberto Salvador Alfredo Jorge Blanco disappeared into the jungle as mysteriously as he had been breathed from it.

The Washington Senators upped the offer to one thousand dollars and a baseball autographed by the whole team. The American State Department hinted darkly that the kidnapping was communist inspired. The CIA air-lifted the government in Santo Domingo twenty-three tanks with which to fight for Esteban's freedom. The government sold half the tanks to Papa Doc Duvalier and declared a Festival Day.

The deadline for execution passed and the wizard did not appear with the uniforms. In America the baseball season was due to open in a few days. The Washington Senators were frantically attempting to trade Esteban Cortizar to a club willing to pay a larger ransom. The owners of the Senators hinted broadly that the New York Yankees were probably behind the kidnapping, after the Yankees offered two of their superstars and a player to be named later in return for Esteban.

The Senators, in the meantime, refused to sign Julio to a new contract. "What do we want with a catcher who can't hit? Let's wait and see if we get Esteban back alive."

In return for his release Esteban offered to buy enough medical supplies for the whole guerilla army; when that offer was refused he offered to buy guns and ship them to the Dominican Republic as medical supplies.

"Shoot him!" said the guerilla leader.

But he could not assemble a volunteer firing squad. Esteban Cortizar, in spite of playing his baseball in America, was a hero to the rank and file guerillas. Since he had been held captive in the guerilla camp, a make-shift baseball diamond had emerged from the jungle. Dense rain forest melted away, and the foul lines and base paths were illuminated by rows of tropical flowers, some white as wedding gowns, others indigo and orchid. The pitcher's rubber was a bar of golden poppies. Since they had no bats, the guerilla soldiers used their rifles, holding them by the barrels, swinging with verve as Esteban twirled the one battered baseball which emerged from some irregular's duffel bag. A sandbag served as catcher, since none of the soldiers would even attempt to catch Esteban's sidearm curve, or his seething fastball. There were a number of rather serious accidents involving batters who forgot to unload their bat.

The guerilla leader appointed a firing squad from the ranks of the non-baseball players. He stood Esteban Cortizar, the world's greatest living baseball player, against an adobe wall, and gave the order for the squad to raise their rifles.

"If you please," said Esteban in a strong voice, "I request to be shot while standing on the pitcher's mound."

A chorus of affirmitive sounds emanated from the assembled guerilla army.

"Very well," said the leader.

Esteban Cortizar stood on the bar of golden poppies, which were soft as velvet beneath his feet, and stared resolutely at the firing squad, which was assembled at home plate. The sky was low and leaden; the trees dripped sullenly. Esteban refused a blindfold.

The leader raised his hand. The firing squad raised their

rifles. Suddenly the air was filled with a sibilation, as if a million swords were slicing the sky.

The guerilla leader lowered his hand slowly, so slowly that the firing squad was not certain if he was giving the signal to fire, or if he was just lowering his hand. Three discharged their guns. Three didn't. From the barrels of the three fired weapons there dropped three blood-red hibiscus, which lay in front of home plate quivering like fresh-caught fish.

As Esteban and the army watched, the wizard descended through the clouds in a blue teardrop of a balloon, of such colour that those who remembered the sky recalled it as being less perfect than the blue of the balloon.

Two more balloons followed, one red as the trembling hibiscus, the other orange as the sun. Beneath each balloon, the wicker gondola was piled high with exotic uniforms, while in the lead balloon the wizard was arrayed in the most magnificent uniform of all, one which caused some of the guerillas to salivate, others to develop erections of magnificent proportions.

During the last days of Esteban's captivity, the Washington Senators decided to trade Julio Cortizar. They didn't expect to get much in return, but they had a power-hitting catcher named Hogarth who had been languishing in Triple A for three years. When Julio's availability was announced the Yankees immediately appeared, their negotiators grinning sagely from behind curved lips. Over the screams of the Senators' manager, Julio was traded to the Yankees for a utility infielder who batted as though he was trying to sponge something dry with his bat.

What the owners of the Senators had never understood was the magnitude of the esoteric game of catch in which the Cortizar brothers engaged. As he grew older Esteban was able to remember the batters he had faced in the womb. He recalled them as being grey and spectral, faceless as fog.

When Esteban began pitching in the Major Leagues, he treated all batters as if seen in the transluscent memory of his mother's womb. When reporters inquired as to how he pitched to a certain batter, he replied that he did not know one hitter from another. When the press asked Julio what pitches he called he would shrug and say, "Esteban knows what pitches he should throw." When pressed further he would admit, "By reading Esteban's mind I always know what pitch is coming."

"If Esteban is released unharmed," the owners told the press, "he'll simply have to learn to throw to whoever is catching."

The wizard, after supplying the guerilla army with uniforms, flew directly to Miami, carrying Esteban, dressed in ill-fitting army fatigues and needing a haircut, but in time for the Senators' home opener.

Esteban did not argue when told his brother had been traded.

"I cannot pitch to anyone but Julio," he said simply. "We go back a long way together."

Since he didn't protest dramatically, management paid no attention.

As Esteban warmed up for the opening game by pitching to the rookie Hogarth, a perplexed pitching coach noticed that every time Esteban threw the sidearm curve, a black-petaled narcissus exploded into Hogarth's mitt. By the time the game started, Hogarth was ankle-deep in soft, black petals, and near hysteria.

Esteban lasted four innings, appeared to make few unusual pitches, but Hogarth was charged with eight passed balls. The fans literally booed Hogarth off the field.

"He crosses me up every time," Hogarth screamed at the manager. "I signal fastball; he okays it, then pitches a curve low and away. He throws whatever he wants, as if I can read his mind."

"Is this true?" the manager asked Esteban.

"I told you I can pitch to no one but Julio." he said quietly.

After Esteban lost his first four starts, the Senators decided to buy Julio back from the Yankees, where he had been relegated to bullpen catcher and was not even allowed to take batting practice.

The Yankees craftily demanded that the Senators trade

Esteban to *them*. The Senators refused. The Yankees offered a quality infielder, a first-string outfielder, two first-round draft picks, two players to be named later, and one million dollars. The Senators refused; they demanded the return of Julio Cortizar. So it came to pass that the Yankees traded a mediocre catcher with a .189 lifetime batting average, to Washington, for an all-star second baseman, their entire first-string outfield, and Hogarth, who was an all-star for seven of his fifteen seasons with the Yankees.

Esteban hurled a three-hit shutout the first time he and Julio were reunited, but the strength was gone from the Washington lineup, and they were never again pennant contenders.

It was Julio who made the decision to retire from baseball.

Even as a child in the Dominican Republic, he was serious and studious, wanting to discuss with the wizard questions of philosophical magnitude. Rather than discussing how to pick a runner off first base he was interested in questions of religious significance. Julio often went to view the priest. The most recent government, when it came to power, had, at great expense, imprisoned the local priest by installing fourteen foot chain link fencing around his manse. In fact, most of the priests in the Dominican Republic suffered a similar fate. Julio would go and stand outside the frosty-bright fence and watch the old priest walk, hands behind back, black cassock sweeping the ground, his stride ungainly, lumbering like a tall, mangy bear. The priest occasionally blessed a goat or a peasant who came close to the fence. Julio noted that the priest's eyes were rheumy and his teeth bad.

"Why doesn't God melt down the fence?" Julio asked the wizard.

"Why should He?" asked the wizard.

"Because the priest is God's representative. He does God's work."

"What can the priest do on the outside that he cannot do inside the fence, except graveside services? If he wished to, he could lead prayers, perform marriages, administer the Eucharist, hear confessions; the sick could be brought to visit

him. Because this priest chooses to decay before your eyes, to
choose as his only duties the blessing of goats and lottery
tickets, is not the fault of God. If I were God I would turn the
fence to stone so the priest might disintegrate in private.''

"I have decided to be a priest," said Julio. "And I will do
the same work no matter which side of the fence I am on."

"You will go far," said the wizard. "I will see that you get to
bless each new balloon that I add to my fleet." The wizard, at
that time, did not own even one balloon.

As time passed Julio became more and more interested in
the philosophical and metaphysical side of life. He was haunted
by the image of the old priest enclosed behind frosty chain link
fencing. Julio supposed his decision to retire had something to
do with the acclaim Esteban received. At press conferences
Julio felt he might as well be a part of the furniture: reporters
seldom spoke to him, then only in a condescending manner,
usually to confirm something Esteban had said, in spite of the
fact that it was Julio who had learned to speak English, Latin,
French, and Italian.

During their twentieth season in the major leagues, when
everyone but the wizard and their mother and father thought
they were thirty-six years old, Julio decided he had had
enough. He had been studying for the priesthood in the off-
season for several years and was nearly ready for ordination.

Esteban, while moderate in most of his habits, was gregar-
ious and outgoing, and loved the attention he received from the
media. He was particularly fond of women and never turned a
Baseball Sadie away unsatisfied. On the other hand, Julio
became accustomed to being ignored: when they were younger
he wished he and Esteban might have been identical twins so
he could have impersonated Esteban occasionally. Julio found
himself uncomfortable with even the most aggressive groupie,
and had been celibate for over five years prior to his retirement.

Esteban won over three hundred games during his career,
and would have won more if he had not played for a perennial
second division team. The twins retired to the replica of the
White House. When Esteban returned to his native land he

was accompanied by four women, all beautiful, all natural blonde, none of whom could speak a word of Spanish, and all of whom were pregnant.

Fernandella was happy at the prospect of a houseful of grandchildren. Fernandella's youngest was now nearly two years of age, and she sometimes lost track of the number of her children, as the father of the twins had never stopped hoping for, and trying to produce another set of magical offspring.

The wizard, even though he was now President of the Republic, still booked bets on baseball games with the father of the twins. The wizard calculated that his winnings paid for the precious metals on his uniforms.

Esteban brought his women to the office of the President of the Republic so the wizard might examine their bellies.

"An infield," said the wizard, smiling, after he had poked and prodded the quartet of taut-skinned beauties. "First base, second base, third base, shortstop," he proclaimed. "The greatest infield in all the history of baseball. And they will be born on the day their father is inducted into the Baseball Hall of Fame."

"But I am not eligible for induction for nearly five years," said an alarmed Esteban.

"This infield will be worth waiting for," said the wizard, ending his audience.

Esteban called his women, not by name but by their place of origin: I-owa, I-DA-ho, Tenn-Essee, and the Blessed Virginia. The women grew to full term, and waited, and waited, and waited. They went for a walk each afternoon in the rose garden, accompanied by Esteban, parading in single file, pale and beautiful, looking like magazine models displaying maternity clothes.

The wizard became President of the Dominican Republic by overthrowing the government, who had been the guerillas at the time of Esteban's kidnapping. The wizard knew the secret of adequate government, which was the delegation of authority; he also knew there was no such thing as good government.

After he had been in power for four years, about two years longer than the average government, his regime was overthrown by the former President, who was also the former and present leader of the guerillas. What the guerilla leader did not count on was that even though the Wizard's regime was deposed, there was no great anger directed at the wizard and no calls for his execution. The wizard had delegated authority so well that he was looked upon as a somewhat benevolent dictator. Great crowds gathered whenever the wizard's fleet of hot-air balloons loomed on the horizon. The guerilla leader knew a politically advantageous situation when he saw one. He appointed the wizard President For Life, a position which had not brought great harm to Haiti's Papa Doc Duvalier, or the somewhat slow-witted son who succeeded him.

As the time for Esteban's eligibility for the Baseball Hall of Fame approached, there was a frenzy of activity in and around Santo Domingo. The wizard hissed from one end of the island to the other making plans for celebrations. He announced amnesty for several thousand political prisoners; he allowed the surviving priests to come out of hiding, providing they stayed behind chain link fence. Esteban was seen in Santo Domingo's finest department stores, buying large, stuffed toys and miniature baseball uniforms. The father of the twins had secretly been in touch with the producers of *That's Incredible*, and *Ripley's Believe It Or Not*.

But the festivities had to be postponed for at least a year when Esteban fell three votes short of election on the first ballot and was not elected as everyone had expected. His non-election generated only mild interest on the sports pages, for Esteban, while being the complete baseball player, was, after all, a foreigner, and a foreigner who had not bothered to learn much English and who had returned to his native country after his retirement.

"Ah," sighed the wizard, who now called himself Pedro Angel Guilermo Cayetano Umberto Salvador Alfredo Jorge Blanco, "if only Esteban could have died like Roberto Clemente. Clemente was so lucky to die while on a mission of mercy at the height of his career. About the only mistake I have ever made," mused the wizard, "was not letting the insurgents execute Esteban Cortizar."

Esteban's women groaned in disappointment. The wizard considered invading Florida.

"What if I am never elected?" wailed Esteban.

"Trust me," said the wizard, who, several times during the next year burned condor dung at odd hours of the day and night.

On his second year of eligibility Esteban was elected with a sizeable majority.

The morning of the day Esteban Cortizar was to be inducted into the Baseball Hall of Fame dawned clear and sparkling as the new crystal-with-rubies epaulets on the shoulders of the President for Life of the Dominican Republic. Esteban elected to stay in the Dominican Republic; he wired the Hall of Fame that pressing business obligations prevented him from attending his inauguration. Actually, he was at the collective bedsides of his four women, waiting for the birth of his infield. The nursery in the replica of the White House was laid out like a baseball field with a crib stationed where each base ought to be.

At precisely 10:00 a.m. a fleet of hot-air balloons rose like tropical birds from the jungle outside of Santo Domingo. The air was permeated by the hiss of the balloons, gentle as baby's breath. The balloons were all perfectly round, shaped and coloured to look exactly like baseballs. Some of the gondolas were filled with tropical flowers: long red lilies, violet and lemon-coloured orchids with petals soft as fragrant velvet. Other gondolas were filled with waving greenery, tough, spindley grasses, carniverous plants testing the air for food.

President for Life, Pedro Angel Guilermo Cayetano Umberto Salvador Alfredo Jorge Blanco, and the former President and guerilla leader stood side by side in the gondola beneath the lead balloon, each bedecked in uniforms so stupifyingly gaudy that only Science Fiction could do them justice.

The one unhappy note on this occasion for jubilance was that the American newspapers all but ignored the eight-page press release, issued on the thick, cream-coloured stationery of the President for Life of the Dominican Republic.

The *Washington Post* condensed the eight pages to five short lines:

Santo Domingo: Dominican Republic President Pedro Blanco bestowed the Order of Great Knight Commander on former Baseball star Esteban Cortizar in honour of his induction to the Baseball Hall of Fame.

"Americans have no sense of tradition or of spectacle," the wizard sniffed, discarding the newspaper. Besides ignoring his titles and names, the paper had reported only one of the titles bestowed on Esteban. Following Great Knight Commander, there was Head of the Civil Service Defence Corps, Honorable Air Commodore, Defender of the Avocado, Commander-in-Chief of the Garment Worker's Union, plus seven more titles.

In the rose garden, the wizard led the singing of the *Himno Nacional*. "Brave Quisqueyanos, let us sing our anthem with deep emotion," the wizard sang, while above the mansion nine baseball-shaped balloons sketched an ethereal diamond in the purest of blue skies.

From inside the mansion the wizard's ears discerned the sound of babies crying, a grandmother fussing, a father's chest expanding, a grandfather's brain plotting.

The wizard breathed the fragrance of the roses, observed the blue fish darting in the frothing stream, watched the two dozen lemon-and-white cockatoos perched in a row on the rose garden fence, and smiling benevolently at all present decided that when the time was right he himself would negotiate the contracts for The Infield.

The Thrill of the Grass

The Thrill of the Grass

1981: the summer the baseball players went on strike. The dull weeks drag by, the summer deepens, the strike is nearly a month old. Outside the city the corn rustles and ripens in the sun. Summer without baseball: a disruption to the psyche. An unexplainable aimlessness engulfs me. I stay later and later each evening in the small office at the rear of my shop. Now, driving home after work, the worst of the rush hour traffic over, it is the time of evening I would normally be heading for the stadium.

I enjoy arriving an hour early, parking in a far corner of the lot, walking slowly toward the stadium, rays of sun dropping softly over my shoulders like tangerine ropes, my shadow gliding with me, black as an umbrella. I like to watch young families beside their campers, the mothers in shorts, grilling hamburgers, their men drinking beer. I enjoy seeing little boys dressed in the home team uniform, barely toddling, clutching hotdogs in upraised hands.

I am a failed shortstop. As a young man, I saw myself diving to my left, graceful as a toppling tree, fielding high grounders like a cat leaping for butterflies, bracing my right foot and tossing to first, the throw true as if a steel ribbon connected my hand and the first baseman's glove. I dreamed of leading the American League in hitting — being inducted into the Hall of Fame. I batted .217 in my senior year of high school and averaged 1.3 errors per nine innings.

I know the stadium will be deserted; nevertheless I wheel my car down off the freeway, park, and walk across the silent lot, my footsteps rasping and mournful. Strangle-grass and creeping charlie are already inching up through the gravel, surreptitious, surprised at their own ease. Faded bottle caps, rusted bits of chrome, an occasional paper clip, recede into the earth. I circle a ticket booth, sun-faded, empty, the door closed by an oversized padlock. I walk beside the tall, machinery-green, board fence. A half mile away a few cars hiss along the freeway; overhead a single-engine plane fizzes lazily. The whole place is silent as an empty classroom, like a house suddenly without children.

It is then that I spot the door-shape. I have to check twice to be sure it is there: a door cut in the deep green boards of the fence, more the promise of a door than the real thing, the kind of door, as children, we cut in the sides of cardboard boxes with our mother's paring knives. As I move closer, a golden circle of lock, like an acrimonious eye, establishes its certainty.

I stand, my nose so close to the door I can smell the faint odour of paint, the golden eye of a lock inches from my own eyes. My desire to be inside the ballpark is so great that for the first time in my life I commit a criminal act. I have been a locksmith for over forty years. I take the small tools from the pocket of my jacket, and in less time than it would take a speedy runner to circle the bases I am inside the stadium. Though the ballpark is open-air, it smells of abandonment; the walkways and seating areas are cold as basements. I breathe the odours of rancid popcorn and wilted cardboard.

The maintenance staff were laid off when the strike began. Synthetic grass does not need to be cut or watered. I stare down at the ball diamond, where just to the right of the pitcher's mound, a single weed, perhaps two inches high, stands defiant in the rain-pocked dirt.

The field sits breathless in the orangy glow of the evening sun. I stare at the potato-coloured earth of the infield, that wide, dun arc, surrounded by plastic grass. As I contemplate the prickly turf, which scorches the thighs and buttocks of a sliding player as if he were being seared by hot steel, it stares back in its uniform ugliness. The seams that send routinely hit ground balls veering at tortuous angles, are vivid, grey as scars.

I remember the ballfields of my childhood, the outfields full of soft hummocks and brown-eyed gopher holes.

I stride down from the stands and walk out to the middle of the field. I touch the stubble that is called grass, take off my shoes, but find it is like walking on a row of toothbrushes. It was an evil day when they stripped the sod from this ballpark, cut it into yard-wide swathes, rolled it, memories and all, into great green-and-black cinnamonroll shapes, trucked it away. Nature temporarily defeated. But Nature is patient.

Over the next few days an idea forms within me, ripening, swelling, pushing everything else into a corner. It is like knowing a new, wonderful joke and not being able to share. I need an accomplice.

I go to see a man I don't know personally, though I have seen his face peering at me from the financial pages of the local newspaper, and the *Wall Street Journal*, and I have been watching his profile at the baseball stadium, two boxes to the right of me, for several years. He is a fan. Really a fan. When the weather is intemperate, or the game not close, the people around us disappear like flowers closing at sunset, but we are always there until the last pitch. I know he is a man who attends because of the beauty and mystery of the game, a man who can sit during the last of the ninth with the game decided innings ago, and draw joy from watching the first baseman adjust the angle of his glove as the pitcher goes into his windup.

He, like me, is a first-base-side fan. I've always watched baseball from behind first base. The positions fans choose at sporting events are like politics, religion, or philosophy: a view of the world, a way of seeing the universe. They make no sense to anyone, have no basis in anything but stubbornness.

I brought up my daughters to watch baseball from the first-base side. One lives in Japan and sends me box scores from Japanese newspapers, and Japanese baseball magazines with pictures of superstars politely bowing to one another. She has a season ticket in Yokohama; on the first-base side.

"Tell him a baseball fan is here to see him," is all I will say to his secretary. His office is in a skyscraper, from which he can look out over the city to where the prairie rolls green as mountain water to the limits of the eye. I wait all afternoon in the artificially cool, glassy reception area with its yellow and mauve chairs, chrome and glass coffee tables. Finally, in the late afternoon, my message is passed along.

"I've seen you at the baseball stadium," I say, not introducing myself.

"Yes," he says. "I recognize you. Three rows back, about eight seats to my left. You have a red scorebook and you often bring your daughter . . ."

"Granddaughter. Yes, she goes to sleep in my lap in the late innings, but she knows how to calculate an ERA and she's only in Grade 2."

"One of my greatest regrets," says this tall man, whose moustache and carefully styled hair are polar-bear white, "is that my grandchildren all live over a thousand miles away. You're very lucky. Now, what can I do for you?"

"I have an idea," I say. "One that's been creeping toward me like a first baseman when the bunt sign is on. What do you think about artificial turf?"

"Hmmmf," he snorts, "that's what the strike should be about. Baseball is meant to be played on summer evenings and Sunday afternoons, on grass just cut by a horse-drawn mower," and we smile as our eyes meet.

"I've discovered the ballpark is open, to me anyway," I go on. "There's no one there while the strike is on. The wind blows through the high top of the grandstand, whining until the pigeons in the rafters flutter. It's lonely as a ghost town."

"And what is it you do there, alone with the pigeons?"

"I dream."

"And where do I come in?"

"You've always struck me as a man who dreams. I think we have things in common. I think you might like to come with me. I could show you what I dream, paint you pictures, suggest what might happen . . ."

He studies me carefully for a moment, like a pitcher trying to decide if he can trust the sign his catcher has just given him.

"Tonight?" he says. "Would tonight be too soon?"

"Park in the northwest corner of the lot about 1:00 a.m.. There is a door about fifty yards to the right of the main gate. I'll open it when I hear you."

He nods.

I turn and leave.

The night is clear and cotton warm when he arrives. "Oh, my," he says, staring at the stadium turned chrome-blue by a full moon. "Oh, my," he says again, breathing in the faint odours of baseball, the reminder of fans and players not long gone.

"Let's go down to the field," I say. I am carrying a cardboard pizza box, holding it on the upturned palms of my hands, like an offering.

When we reach the field, he first stands on the mound, makes an awkward attempt at a windup, then does a little sprint from first to about half-way to second. "I think I know what you've brought," he says, gesturing toward the box, "but let me see anyway."

I open the box in which rests a square foot of sod, the grass smooth and pure, cool as a swatch of satin, fragile as baby's hair.

"Ohhh," the man says, reaching out a finger to test the moistness of it. "Oh, I see."

We walk across the field, the harsh, prickly turf making the bottoms of my feet tingle, to the left-field corner where, in the angle formed by the foul line and the warning track, I lay down the square foot of sod. "That's beautiful," my friend says, kneeling beside me, placing his hand, fingers spread wide, on the verdant square, leaving a print faint as a veronica.

I take from my belt a sickle-shaped blade, the kind used for cutting carpet. I measure along the edge of the sod, dig the point in and pull carefully toward me. There is a ripping sound, like tearing an old bed sheet. I hold up the square of artificial turf like something freshly killed, while all the time digging the sharp point into the packed earth I have exposed. I replace the sod lovingly, covering the newly bared surface.

"A protest," I say.

"But it could be more," the man replies.

"I hoped you'd say that. It could be. If you'd like to come back . . ."

"Tomorrow night?"

"Tomorrow night would be fine. But there will be an admission charge . . ."

"A square of sod?"

"A square of sod two inches thick . . ."

"Of the same grass?"

"Of the same grass. But there's more."

"I suspected as much."

"You must have a friend . . ."

"Who would join us?"

"Yes."

"I have two. Would that be all right?"

"I trust your judgement."

"My father. He's over eighty," my friend says. "You might have seen him with me once or twice. He lives over fifty miles from here, but if I call him he'll come. And my friend . . ."

"If they pay their admission they'll be welcome . . ."

"And *they* may have friends . . ."

"Indeed they may. But what will we do with this?" I say, holding up the sticky-backed square of turf, which smells of glue and fabric.

"We could mail them anonymously to baseball executives, politicians, clergymen."

"Gentle reminders not to tamper with Nature."

We dance toward the exit, rampant with excitement.

"You will come back? You'll bring others?"

"Count on it," says my friend.

They do come, those trusted friends, and friends of friends, each making a live, green deposit. At first, a tiny row of sod squares begins to inch along toward left-centre field. The next night even more people arrive, the following night more again, and the night after there is positively a crowd. Those who come once seem always to return accompanied by friends, occasionally a son or young brother, but mostly men my age or older, for we are the ones who remember the grass.

Night after night the pilgrimage continues. The first night I stand inside the deep green door, listening. I hear a vehicle stop; hear a car door close with a snug thud. I open the door when the sound of soft soled shoes on gravel tells me it is time. The door swings silent as a snake. We nod curt greetings to each other. Two men pass me, each carrying a grasshopper legged sprinkler. Later, each sprinkler will sizzle like frying onions as it wheels, a silver sparkler in the moonlight.

During the nights that follow, I stand sentinel-like at the top of the grandstand, watching as my cohorts arrive. Old men walking across a parking lot in a row, in the dark, carrying coiled hoses, looking like the many wheels of a locomotive, old men who have slipped away from their homes, skulked down their sturdy sidewalks, breathing the cool, grassy, after-midnight air. They have left behind their sleeping, grey-haired women, their immaculate bungalows, their manicured lawns. They continue to walk across the parking lot, while occasionally a soft wheeze, a nibbling, breathy sound like an old horse might make, divulges their humanity. They move methodically toward the baseball stadium which hulks against the moon-blue sky like a small mountain. Beneath the tint of starlight, the tall light standards which rise above the fences and grandstand glow purple, necks bent forward, like sunflowers heavy with seed.

My other daughter lives in this city, is married to a fan, but one who watches baseball from behind third base. And like marrying outside the faith, she has been converted to the third-base side. They have their own season tickets, twelve rows up just to the outfield side of third base. I love her, but I don't trust her enough to let her in on my secret.

I could trust my granddaughter, but she is too young. At her age she shouldn't have to face such responsibility. I remember my own daughter, the one who lives in Japan, remember her at nine, all knees, elbows and missing teeth — remember peering in her room, seeing her asleep, a shower of well-thumbed base-ball cards scattered over her chest and pillow.

I haven't been able to tell my wife — it is like my compat-riots and I are involved in a ritual for true believers only. Maggie, who knew me when I still dreamed of playing profes-sionally myself — Maggie, after over half a lifetime together, comes and sits in my lap in the comfortable easy chair which has adjusted through the years to my thickening shape, just as she has. I love to hold the lightness of her, her tongue exploring my mouth, gently as a baby's finger.

"Where do you go?" she asks sleepily when I crawl into bed at dawn.

I mumble a reply. I know she doesn't sleep well when I'm gone. I can feel her body rhythms change as I slip out of bed after midnight.

"Aren't you too old to be having a change of life," she says, placing her toast-warm hand on my cold thigh.

I am not the only one with this problem.

"I'm developing a reputation," whispers an affable man at the ballpark. "I imagine any number of private investigators following any number of cars across the city. I imagine them creeping about the parking lot, shining pen-lights on licence plates, trying to guess what we're up to. Think of the reports they must prepare. I wonder if our wives are disappointed that we're not out discoing with frizzy-haired teenagers?"

Night after night, virtually no words are spoken. Each man seems to know his assignment. Not all bring sod. Some carry rakes, some hoes, some hoses, which, when joined together, snake across the infield and outfield, dispensing the blessing of water. Others, cradle in their arms bags of earth for building up the infield to meet the thick, living sod.

I often remain high in the stadium, looking down on the men moving over the earth, dark as ants, each sodding, cutting, watering, shaping. Occasionally the moon finds a knife blade as it trims the sod or slices away a chunk of artificial turf, and tosses the reflection skyward like a bright ball. My body tingles. There should be symphony music playing. Everyone should be humming "America The Beautiful."

Toward dawn, I watch the men walking away in groups, like small patrols of soldiers, carrying instead of arms, the tools and utensils which breathe life back into the arid ballfield.

Row by row, night by night, we lay the little squares of sod, moist as chocolate cake with green icing. Where did all the sod come from? I picture many men, in many parts of the city, surreptitiously cutting chunks out of their own lawns in the leafy midnight darkness, listening to the uncomprehending protests of their wives the next day — pretending to know nothing of it — pretending to have called the police to investigate.

When the strike is over I know we will all be here to watch the workouts, to hear the recalcitrant joints crackling like twigs after the forced inactivity. We will sit in our regular seats, scattered like popcorn throughout the stadium, and we'll nod as we pass on the way to the exits, exchange secret smiles, proud as new fathers.

For me, the best part of all will be the surprise. I feel like a magician who has gestured hypnotically and produced an elephant from thin air. I know I am not alone in my wonder. I know that rockets shoot off in half-a-hundred chests, the excitement of birthday mornings, Christmas eves, and home-town doubleheaders, boils within each of my conspirators. Our secret rites have been performed with love, like delivering a valentine to a sweetheart's door in that blue-steel span of morning just before dawn.

Players and management are meeting round the clock. A settlement is imminent. I have watched the stadium covered square foot by square foot until it looks like green graph paper. I have stood and felt the cool odours of the grass rise up and touch my face. I have studied the lines between each small square, watched those lines fade until they were visible to my eyes alone, then not even to them.

What will the players think, as they straggle into the stadium and find the miracle we have created? The old-timers will raise their heads like ponies, as far away as the parking lot, when the thrill of the grass reaches their nostrils. And, as they dress, they'll recall sprawling in the lush outfields of childhood, the grass as cool as a mother's hand on a forehead.

"Goodbye, goodbye," we say at the gate, the smell of water, of sod, of sweat, small perfumes in the air. Our secrets are safe with each other. We go our separate ways.

Alone in the stadium in the last chill darkness before dawn, I drop to my hands and knees in the centre of the outfield. My palms are sodden. Water touches the skin between my spread fingers. I lower my face to the silvered grass, which, wonder of wonders, already has the ephemeral odours of baseball about it.